She felt good against him. Warm and soft and very feminine.

He didn't want to let her go.

"Connor?"

The lipstick she'd applied earlier had long since worn off, yet her lips were still rosy and moist. They were slightly parted in question, giving him just a glimpse of teeth and tongue.

He swallowed.

She must have picked up on the emotions suddenly running through him. Her eyes narrowed and darkened. A low groan wedged in his throat.

"Connor?" Mia said again, her voice little more than a whisper this time.

Maybe later he would come up with a good excuse for his actions. At least an explanation. But for now…

He lowered his head and captured her mouth with his.

Dear Reader,

When our daughter, Kerry, entered medical school, we knew it would be challenging. None of us realized exactly how much so. It wasn't only that the class-work was difficult, but so much of it was thrown at them all at once. Little time was left for former friends and activities. Kerry received her MD in May. She has recently begun a five-year residency program for a career in child psychiatry.

When I told her I was considering a series about a group of medical students, she was intrigued and offered lots of anecdotes and information for me to use. This book and the others that will follow are entirely fictional, of course, but Kerry gave me quite a few ideas. She read *Diagnosis: Daddy* as soon as I finished it and assured me that I accurately conveyed the stress and the guilt experienced by many first-year medical students. I considered that high praise, indeed!

I hope you enjoy the tale of how medical student and single dad Connor Hayes finds enduring love with his best friend, Mia, despite all the challenges they face along the way.

Gina Wilkins

DIAGNOSIS: DADDY

GINA WILKINS

SPECIAL EDITION®

Published by Silhouette Books

America's Publisher of Contemporary Romance

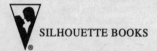

SILHOUETTE BOOKS

ISBN-13: 978-0-373-65472-7

DIAGNOSIS: DADDY

Recycling programs
for this product may
not exist in your area.

GINA WILKINS

is a bestselling and award-winning author who has written more than seventy novels for Harlequin and Silhouette Books. She credits her successful career in romance to her long, happy marriage and her three "extraordinary" children.

A lifelong resident of central Arkansas, Ms. Wilkins sold her first book to Harlequin in 1987 and has been writing full-time since. She has appeared on the Waldenbooks, B. Dalton and *USA TODAY* bestseller lists. She is a three-time recipient of the Maggie Award for Excellence, sponsored by Georgia Romance Writers, and has won several awards from the reviewers of *Romantic Times BOOKreviews*.

For Dr. Kerry Wilkins Snook. I'm so proud of you.
Thanks for all your help.

Chapter One

"You look terrible."

Connor Hayes grimaced and ran a hand through his tousled hair. "Thanks a lot, Mia. I can always count on you to boost my ego."

Maybe she had been a little blunt, but Mia Doyle wasn't about to take back her words. As attractive as her friend was, he looked pretty ragged at the moment. His sandy hair was in dire need of a trim, his navy blue eyes were red-rimmed and bleary, and he had the grayish pallor of someone who hadn't seen the sun in several days. He was only thirty, but she suspected anyone meeting him for the first time today would probably guess him to be a few years older. "When's the last time you had a full night's sleep?"

"Define 'full.'"

"More than four hours."

"Hmm…it's been a while," he admitted.

She sighed and shook her head. "Really, Connor, you can't go on like this. You have to get some rest."

"I will," he assured her. "After this test tomorrow. It's going to be a killer."

"They're all killers," she reminded him, setting a plate of food in front of him. She had to push a pile of books, notebooks and papers out of the way to find a spot on his kitchen table for the plate. "Don't you think you'll perform better on the test if you're rested and fresh?"

He sighed heavily and gripped the fork she thrust into his hand. "Probably."

"But you'll still sit up most of the night studying," she concluded in resignation.

The smile he gave her was sheepish. "Yeah. Probably."

Shaking her head, she cleared off a few inches of table for her own plate. She had brought a chicken and broccoli casserole, filling and healthy. Knowing the grueling schedule her friend and former coworker was enduring during his first year of medical school, she had gotten into the habit of bringing meals to him a couple of times a week. Sometimes she quizzed him for upcoming exams, using study guides and practice tests from his stacks of materials. He seemed to enjoy her company during his near-total exile from his former social life.

She worried about him not taking good care of himself because of his obsession with doing well in medical school. And she missed seeing him every day at work, sharing lunches and class prep times together, bonding over stories of their most difficult students. This school year just hadn't been the same without Connor there to greet her every morning with a smile and a bad joke.

They had been friends for more than three years, having both been teachers at a nearby Little Rock, Arkansas, high school. Mia taught advanced placement literature classes; Connor had taught health and physical education and had been an assistant coach for the football team. Early in their friendship, he had confessed that he wanted to attend medical school. He'd worried that he'd waited too long to even try, but she'd encouraged—well, nagged him into taking the MCAT and applying to medical school. No one had been happier for him when he'd been accepted, even though she knew it would change their relationship significantly.

"This is really good, Mia. Thanks."

She smiled wryly as he shoveled casserole into his mouth. He was eating as if he'd forgotten all about food until now. She suspected that he'd done just that. She didn't bother to ask when he'd last had a complete meal. Judging by the evidence she'd seen scattered around the kitchen and in the overflowing wastebasket beneath the sink, he'd been living on TV dinners and energy bars since she'd last brought him a meal, three days earlier.

"More iced tea?" she asked.

"I'll get it."

But she was already on her feet. She refilled his glass and then her own before putting the pitcher back in the fridge.

"Thanks," he murmured, lifting the glass to his lips.

"You're welcome. Is there anything I can do to help you study after you've eaten? I'd be happy to quiz you."

He looked at her somberly across the table. "You're too good to me. Especially because I've been neglecting you so badly lately. I even forgot to call you on your birthday."

He had apologized profusely and repeatedly for that slip as soon as he realized what he'd done—two days after the actual event. Although she had been painfully aware that he hadn't called on the day itself, she'd understood. He was overwhelmed with the sheer amount of information being thrown at him on a daily basis, and which he was expected to retain and be tested on at regular intervals. They had expected that the first year of medical school would be grueling, but they'd both been surprised by the arduous reality.

It was insane, they agreed. Certainly not the most efficient method of training new doctors, in their studied opinion—but it was difficult to break through the prevailing argument that "it's always been done this way." So all he could do was dig in and prove he had the endurance and stubbornness to make it through the first year, which seemed to be the main point of the curriculum.

"Stop apologizing about the birthday, okay? I completely understand. You had that big gross anatomy exam that afternoon and no one could blame you for being totally preoccupied by that."

He shook his head with a rueful smile. "You're still letting me off too easy. Med school is no excuse to blow off the best friend I've ever had."

She returned the smile, then thought about what he'd said as she finished her meal. Best friends. That was the way they thought of themselves and referred to themselves to others. A slightly unconventional friendship, of course, because he was two years older and they weren't the same gender. Some people seemed to find it hard to believe that a man and a woman could be so close without being physically involved, but she and Connor had never crossed that particular line for several reasons. Primarily because when they'd first met, he had been in the process of a divorce and in no mood to get romantically involved with anyone else so soon.

By the time his divorce was final and he had recovered somewhat from the ordeal, Mia had been seeing someone, and she and Connor had already settled into a comfortable platonic relationship based on mutual tastes and values and ideals, shared senses of humor and similar big dreams for their futures. Neither of them had wanted to risk doing anything to endanger their treasured camaraderie. So they had endured the gossip and the nosy questions, as well as the annoying suspicions of the unexpectedly possessive man she had dated and then dumped, and their friendship had survived.

They had gotten even closer after the death of his mother almost two years ago. He'd told her then that she'd somehow known just what to say and do to help him handle the grief, even though all she felt she had done was to offer to listen whenever he needed to talk.

She saw no reason for their friendship ever to end. Forgotten birthdays notwithstanding.

"Actually," he said, pushing his emptied plate away and standing. "Wait right here. I've got something for you and now seems as good a time as any to give it to you."

"You didn't have to—"

But he was already gone. She wasn't really startled that he'd gotten her a present because they'd been in the habit of exchanging gifts for the past couple of years. She was more surprised that he'd had time to shop. Maybe he'd ordered something over the Internet.

She had just finished loading the dishwasher with their dinner plates when he returned, a wrapped gift in his hand. "Sorry it's late," he said. "It was delivered just this afternoon."

So he had shopped with the click of a computer key. Still, it was nice that he'd thought of her, and because she knew very well that his money was limited right now, considering he was attending medical school on student loans, it was a very generous gesture. "You really didn't have to get me anything," she repeated, even as she took the gift he offered her.

"I wanted to," he answered simply. "Go ahead. Open it."

"It's heavy." Setting the book-size box on the table, she pulled off the inexpensive red Christmas bow he'd stuck to the red-and-green plaid wrapping paper that also looked suspiciously Christmasy. Never mind that it was October; this was probably the only wrapping paper he'd had on hand, most likely left over from last year's holidays.

Finally finding the gift beneath all the paper and tape he'd applied, she gasped. Lifting the two-volume set from the box, she read the title. "*The Cambridge History of Irish Literature.* Connor."

He looked at her with a hint of nerves in his expression, as if trying to gauge whether she really was pleased with the gift. "I wasn't sure about it, but the reviews sounded good. Like something you might like."

"Are you kidding? This is great. Perfect for my library. But you really shouldn't have spent this much." He had to have spent a couple hundred dollars for this, she thought, touched that he'd gone to the effort to find something so personally tailored to her tastes.

He frowned, as if she'd struck a nerve with her comment about the cost. She knew his ex had departed with everything she could grab when she'd left him for someone else, and it had taken him a while to recover financially. The little house and an aging compact car were his only significant material assets for the moment because he was investing everything else into his future medical career.

"I wanted to get you something you'd like," he said. "As much as you've done for me, it's the least I could do in return."

She didn't care for the implication that the gift was payback for her support of his efforts to get into medical school and to do well now that he was in. He probably hadn't really meant it that way, but it was certainly the way it had sounded.

Why were they both so sensitive this evening? She gave an impatient shake of her head, telling herself to snap out of it. She should just appreciate the gift and the thoughts behind it, whatever they had been. "Thank you."

He smiled and gave her a quick, one-armed hug. "You're welcome."

Her heart fluttered a little, but she returned the smile easily. "Go study. I'll clean up in here."

He didn't waste time arguing with her. He hauled a stack of books into the living room and had buried his head inside them before she cleared away the first plate.

It was just as well, she thought with a slight smile, that she wasn't a particularly high-maintenance type of friend. As dear as he was to her, she wasn't blind when it came to Connor's faults. Lately he had been more than a little self-absorbed and decidedly obsessed with his schoolwork. She certainly understood why he needed to be that way at this point in his life, but she knew better than to invest too much of herself with a self-centered, manipulative man. Been there, done that. Still bore the emotional scars.

Connor wasn't anything like Dale had been, but only a true masochist would get involved with a first-year med student, she thought with a wry smile.

His eyes burned so badly that Connor could hardly focus on the charts in front of him. He rubbed his closed eyes with his fingertips, which didn't help.

He needed coffee. Some sort of stimulant to wake him up and sharpen his mind. He'd never get through all these tables tonight without it.

Standing, he walked into the kitchen, limping a little because he'd been sitting in one position for too long. He heard joints crack as he reached for a cup and he felt suddenly older than his thirty years. He hoped there was some coffee left in the insulated carafe he always kept filled. If not, he'd have to waste valuable study time making another pot.

Looking around for it, he noted that the kitchen was immaculate. Gleaming, even. Every scrap of trash was gone, all the dishes washed and put away, the stovetop and counters wiped clean. Even the floor had been swept.

Mia, he thought with a little niggling of guilt. She'd cleaned his kitchen. And he suspected that if he checked his bathroom and bedroom, he'd find that she hadn't restricted her cleaning to this room. On an impulse, he opened the folding wood doors that concealed the washer and dryer at the far end of the kitchen. Clean jeans, T-shirts, socks and underwear were stacked neatly on the dryer. When he opened the dryer, he found a load of clean towels, still warm and fluffy. Apparently she'd had the washer and dryer running the entire time she'd been there that evening. He hadn't even noticed.

Had he even thanked her properly for bringing dinner? He frowned, trying to clearly remember her departure…just over an hour earlier, he thought, glancing at the digital clock on the microwave. He'd been buried in his books, staring intently at a diagram of the cardiovascular system, trying to memorize the vessels that originate from the external carotid artery when she'd told him she was leaving. He remembered looking up and reciting, "The superior thyroid artery, the lingual artery, the facial artery, the occipital artery and the posterior auricular artery."

Without even blinking, Mia had laughed and leaned over to brush a light kiss against his cheek. Her bright blue eyes had been warm in her pretty, girl-next-door face when she'd drawn away, tucking a strand of her light brown hair behind her ear. "Thank you again for the birthday present. Good luck on your test tomorrow. Call me and let me know how it went, okay?"

"Yeah, okay," he had replied, his eyes already on the diagram again as he'd squinted at the brachiocephalic artery, which divided into the common carotid artery and the subclavian artery. "'Night, Mia. Drive carefully."

He distinctly remembered telling her to drive carefully. Not exactly a "thank you so much for all you've done for me tonight and ever since I started med school, I don't know what I would have done without you." But at least it showed he cared about her, right?

He didn't deserve a friend like her, he thought with a disgusted shake of his head. Maybe he could pay her back somehow when she started grad school, which was her plan after teaching and saving for another year or so.

Yeah, right. As a second-year med student, he would take

another full slate of courses and begin studying for Step One of the nightmarish medical licensing exam that had to be passed before he could continue with his training. As tough as his first year had proven to be, there were some who warned that the second year was even more arduous. Hard to imagine.

In his third year, he would begin rotations through various disciplines of medicine, continue with classes, and start seeing real patients. Those rotations, with increasing levels of responsibility, would continue during his fourth year, along with preparation for the Step Two exams—clinical knowledge and clinical skills.

All assuming, of course, that he made it through the rest of this semester.

He might as well face it. He wouldn't be helping anyone but himself for the next three and a half years—and then the four years of residency following that. He would be close to forty by the time he was a full-fledged physician, ready to strike out on his own. What on earth had made him think he could do this—and that the end result would be worth the stress, the sacrifices and the financial investment?

But that was exhaustion talking, he told himself, reaching grimly for the coffee carafe. And nerves. He'd wanted to be a doctor since he was a kid. It was his own fear and stupidity that had kept him from pursuing the goal earlier and he wasn't going to let his dreams be derailed again.

A yellow sticky note was affixed to the carafe. "It's decaf," it read in Mia's looping handwriting. "Get some sleep."

His vague feelings of guilt dissipated and he scowled. He needed caffeine, damn it. Now he would have to make a fresh pot. He opened the lid of the carafe, and the scent of freshly brewed decaf coffee wafted to his nostrils. Mia made really good coffee.

He sighed and filled his cup. So maybe the jolt of the hot liquid alone would sharpen him long enough to finish the review he'd been studying. And she was probably right; he did need a few hours of sleep before he tackled the six-hour-long exam tomorrow.

He really didn't deserve a friend like Mia, he thought again as he carried the steaming mug back to his papers. Someday he was going to have to figure out a way to repay her.

"So have you seen Connor lately?" Spanish teacher Natalie Berman asked as she picked at the school cafeteria lunch of greasy spaghetti, cold green beans, canned fruit cocktail and a rather stale roll.

Wishing she had remembered to pack a lunch that day, Mia swallowed a forkful of green beans before wiping her mouth with a paper towel. "I saw him a couple of nights ago. He was studying for a monster exam and I made him a casserole."

"Is he doing okay?"

Mia shrugged and twisted her fork in the overcooked pasta. "He looks really tired. He could use a solid eight or ten hours of sleep, but I don't think he's going to get that until Christmas break, if he allows himself to rest even then."

Natalie shook her dark head in disapproval. "Can't imagine why he wanted to take that on. He had a good job here. He probably would have been named head coach when Coach Johnson retires next year. Now it's going to be years before Connor finishes school and then he'll have all those loans to pay back. Not that he'll have much trouble doing that," she admitted. "Doctors certainly make good money."

"He didn't go into it for the money. He's pursuing a dream he's had most of his life. And he'll be a great doctor."

"He will," Natalie admitted. "But he was a good teacher, too. And a good coach."

"This is what he wanted."

"And heaven knows you want him to have everything he wants," her friend murmured over a plastic tumbler of watery iced tea. "Just like you do for everyone else you care about. I still say you try too hard to make everyone happy."

"Yes, well, I'm going to be very selfish when I start grad school in the next year or so. Watching Connor has reminded me of how much work it's going to be to take classes and tests again. I'm going to have to concentrate entirely on myself while I earn my doctorate."

Looking skeptical, Natalie crumpled her napkin and tossed it on her plate. "You? Selfish? Yeah, right."

"Just watch me. You'll call and want me to go shopping with you and I'll tell you I can't. Have to study. Or you'll want me to give you a lift to the airport and I'll turn you down flat because I have a paper to write."

"Hmm." It was obvious that Natalie didn't believe a word of her friend's assertion. Even Mia wondered if she would be able to follow through. She'd always had a hard time with that *no* word when it came to people she cared about.

"So, about tomorrow night…"

Mia paused in the process of gathering the remains of her lunch onto the brown plastic tray in preparation for carrying it to the conveyor belt that would sweep it back into the kitchen for cleaning. "What about tomorrow night?"

Natalie sighed loudly and rolled her eyes. "Double date? Me and Donnie and you and…uh, Donnie's friend whose name I've forgotten."

Groaning, Mia sat down again. "I never said I would do that. I said I would think about it."

"C'mon, Mia, it'll be great. Donnie's fun and his friend's probably fun, too."

"Probably?"

"Well, I've never actually met him. But Donnie says he's a great guy."

"And this allegedly great guy needs a date tomorrow night because…?"

"Because he's new in town and doesn't know many people yet. We're just being friendly. You know, welcoming him to town. Southern hospitality—"

"Only extends so far," Mia muttered.

"I'm not asking you to sleep with him or anything. Just join us for dinner. Maybe a movie or something. How bad could it be?"

"You really want me to answer that?"

"Do it for me, okay? Donnie was really pleased when I said I'd bring someone to meet his friend. You don't have to see him again if you don't want to, but at least meet the guy."

Letting out a gusty breath, Mia nodded. "All right. I'll meet him."

Natalie beamed. "Thank you. You'll see, it will be fun."

Mia wasn't so sure. But she hadn't been able to disappoint her friend.

That was going to change, she promised herself. She really was going to learn to say no. Next year.

Mia was getting ready for her double date the next evening when Connor called. "Didn't you have another exam today? How did it go?" she asked.

"As hard as I expected. But I think I did okay on both tests this week."

"I'm sure you did well. When will you know?"

"Middle of next week, I think."

"Did you get any sleep last night?"

"A few hours," he said, notably evasive. "But then I came home after the exam and crashed. Just fell facedown in the bed and slept for three solid hours."

"You needed the rest."

"Yeah, I feel better. Good enough that I might go out for pizza or something tonight. It's been days since I've been out of the house other than to go to class or lab. Want to join me?"

For some reason, it irked her a little that he just assumed she would be free to join him on such short notice. Even though normally she would have been. And would have accepted the last-minute invitation. "I'm sorry, I can't tonight. I have a date."

There was a distinct pause before he responded. "Yeah? Anyone I know?"

"Not even anyone *I* know. Natalie set me up with someone."

"Oh. You, um, trust Natalie's taste in guys?"

"I guess I'll find that out tonight."

"Yeah. I suppose I need to let you get ready. I hope you have a good time."

"I'll certainly try. Thanks. And congratulations on surviving the exams."

"Yeah. I'll talk to you later."

"Sure. Later."

She disconnected the call with a frown. That had been a bit weird. Connor had actually seemed disapproving that she was going out on a blind date. Surely he wasn't annoyed that she'd been unavailable to have pizza with him. If so, then maybe it was time she stopped being quite so available for Connor. Maybe he was starting to take her a bit too much for granted.

Resolutely, she turned to the mirror to finish applying fresh makeup. Tonight could be fun, she reminded herself. This guy Natalie had found for her could be very nice, she could have a great time, they might even want to see each other again. She should really be looking forward to this date.

Unfortunately, she was too keenly aware that she would much rather have been free to go out for pizza with Connor.

Connor joined four of his classmates for a study session Saturday morning. The five of them had met several times to study together during this first semester of medical school. They seemed to click as a group, and their learning styles meshed well. He liked them all and enjoyed working with them, although sometimes he just needed to study alone. Or with Mia.

The thought of Mia made him frown. He wondered how her date had gone the night before.

He was undoubtedly a selfish jerk. He should be pleased that she'd had the chance to go out and have a good time. Like him, Mia tended to be a workaholic. When she wasn't actually teaching, she was preparing for classes or grading papers or doing something nice for a friend. It was rare that she took advantage of an evening just to indulge herself. And while he suspected that her double date last night had been a favor to Natalie, he should still be hoping that she'd had a great time.

Instead, he found himself worrying that she'd had too good a time. For all he knew, she could be with that guy right now. Laughing and flirting and…well, whatever. And he was trying to study, wishing she were with him to light his house with her smile, to cheerfully nag him into eating and taking breaks, to reassure him that he could survive this training and that all the effort and sacrifice would pay off someday.

He really was selfish, he thought again, shaking his head in disapproval. Mia deserved so much more than the distracted friendship that was all he could offer her at the moment. Of course, she had big plans of her own. Grad school was going to take a great deal of her time and energy. Did she really want to start a new romance with this guy Natalie had scrounged up now and risk jeopardizing her own carefully worked-out agenda?

He winced as he realized that he was merely rationalizing his desire for her to stay as single and unattached as he was.

"Hey, Connor. Come on, man, get with the program. You've been a zombie all afternoon."

Connor met Ron Gibson's quizzical gaze apologetically. "I know. Sorry. I think I might be on study overload."

"Who isn't?" Anne Easton asked with a weary sigh. She pushed her pale blond hair out of her face, which was bare of makeup today, making her look even younger than her twenty-three years. Anne was the youngest of the group; Connor was the eldest.

"Anyone want a soda?" James Stillman, their host for today, pushed himself out of his chair at the table and moved toward the fridge. Of all of them, the material came the easiest to James. Maybe because at only twenty-six, he had already obtained a doctorate in microbiology before deciding to attend medical school.

Connor didn't know why James hadn't gone the M.D./Ph.D. route, which would have allowed him to pursue the degrees simultaneously, but he supposed James had simply changed his mind about which career he wanted. While Connor liked James, he had a hard time reading him. Brilliant and affable, James revealed little about himself, even to this group who had become his friends.

"Toss a soda this way," Ron accepted with one of his quick grins. Twenty-five-year-old Ron had messy brown hair, smiling brown eyes, a contagious grin bracketed by dimples and an irrepressible sense of humor that somehow survived even the most grueling session.

Haley Wright, the final member of the group, often grew exasperated with Ron, asking if he took anything seriously. To which Ron always replied, "Only having fun, kiddo. I always take that seriously."

It was a wonder, really, that Ron had fallen in with this generally more-serious group. And yet somehow he, too, just seemed to fit in naturally.

"I'd take some more coffee," Connor said, standing with his empty mug. "I'll get it."

Haley followed him with her own coffee mug, and Anne made herself a second cup of herbal tea. Always the gracious host, James provided everything they needed when they met at his tidy apartment. They'd already devoured the pizzas he'd had delivered at noon. A plate of cookies and a bowl of candy sat in the middle of the paper-strewn, round oak table where they studied, in case anyone needed a sugar jolt.

Popping the top of his soda can, Ron studied Connor's face. "So, is there anything in particular bugging you today? You're not all that worried about the histology exam Monday, are you?"

"I worry about all the exams," Connor answered drily. "But no more for this one than the others. I guess I really am just tired."

"A few more weeks until Thanksgiving," Haley said with a wistful sigh. "Four whole days with no classes or exams. I'm keeping a countdown to give myself incentive until then."

Twenty-six-year-old Haley had honey hair, amber eyes and a firmly pointed little chin that was evidence of her tenacious personality. She was the cheerleader of the group, the one who kept everyone else encouraged and on track. She was the one who called when she sensed they were down, who prodded when she thought they were slacking off, who seemed most delighted when they did well.

Anne, on the other hand, was probably the most competitive of them all. Not because she had a desire to show them up or to always be the best, Connor had decided, but because she seemed to have a need to prove something. To herself? To her family? He didn't know, but he worried about her sometimes. He thought she needed to cut herself a little slack, to allow for mistakes and failures rather than always demanding perfection of herself. She was going to burn out fast if she didn't relax a little, he feared.

As for himself—he just wanted to make it through the first semester. And then the seven semesters after that, one milestone at a time, until he finally held that diploma he'd wanted for so long.

He'd sacrificed a hell of a lot to get to this point, he thought grimly. Thinking again about Mia's date last night, he found himself wondering incongruously if maybe he'd sacrificed too much.

"Okay, guys, back to work," Haley ordered, reaching for a study sheet. "I'll quiz this time."

It was just after four that afternoon when Connor let himself into his house. Just as he closed the door behind him, his telephone rang. He nearly stumbled over himself in his rush to answer it, thinking it might be Mia. He was just casually curious about how her evening had gone, he assured himself even as he snatched up the phone without bothering to check the ID screen. "Hello?"

"Mr. Hayes? Connor Hayes?" It was a man's voice, and one Connor didn't recognize.

"Yes. Who is this?"

"My name is Art Haskell, Mr. Hayes. I'm an attorney and I have something rather significant to discuss with you. Would you be available to meet with me sometime this evening?"

Mia had just settled onto her couch to watch a television program when her doorbell rang at nine o'clock Saturday evening. Setting aside the remote, she automatically brushed a hand over her casual top and jeans as she moved to answer the summons. She wasn't expecting anyone this late, so she checked the peep hole before she opened the door.

A bit surprised to find Connor on her doorstep, she let him in. "Well, hi," she said. "This is an unexpected visit. Why didn't you call? Have you had anything to eat?"

When he didn't respond to her questions, she closed the door and looked at him more closely. What she saw in his face made her stomach clench. "Connor? Are you okay? What's wrong?"

His expression grim, his eyes looking shock-glazed, he swallowed visibly before answering. "I, um, I just came from a meeting with an attorney. I—"

Taking a deep breath, he shoved a hand through his hair before blurting, "I'm going to have to quit medical school."

Chapter Two

Mia stared blankly at Connor, deciding she must have heard him wrong. Surely he hadn't said he was quitting medical school. Not after all he'd gone through to get to this point. "What on earth are you talking about?"

"It's sort of a long story."

"I've got time." Taking hold of his arm, she drew him to the couch. "Let me get you something to drink. Soda? Coffee?"

He shook his head, his expression still heartrending. "No."

Sinking onto the couch beside him, she took his hands in hers. His fingers lay limply in her grasp and his skin felt cold. "Connor, you're scaring me. What's happened?"

His eyes met hers. "I got a call from an attorney this afternoon. He'd been trying to reach me for a couple hours, but I was with the study group. He asked if I could meet with him this evening at his office downtown."

"On a Saturday evening?" She swallowed, thinking that sounded awfully serious. "What was the meeting about?"

He cleared his throat, as though searching for the right words. "I— There was this girl."

She frowned.

"A girl from college," he clarified. "We hooked up during my senior year. I was almost twenty-two, a few months from graduating. I'd been working pretty hard to earn my degree. Brandy was a—well, sort of a flake. Unpredictable. Impulsive. A little crazy, in a passionate, free-spirited sort of way. I guess she was what I needed at the time because I was obsessed with her for a few months. And then she got bored and she took off. After a few weeks of sulking, I realized I was sort of relieved. I'd had fun, but she certainly wasn't someone I wanted to spend my whole life tangled up with, you know?"

Brandy certainly didn't sound like someone Mia would expect Connor to be involved with. But she supposed everyone made a few mistakes when it came to youthful romantic relationships. She had certainly made a couple, herself. She nodded. "Go on."

He moistened his lips. "I got involved with Gretchen a few months later as sort of a rebound from Brandy. Gretchen was everything Brandy wasn't. She was focused and normal and completely predictable. I thought we were perfectly matched. She was a dental assistant and she seemed to be content to be that and a coach's wife. She didn't encourage me to pursue a medical degree and I guess I used her as an excuse not to do so. I think the whole idea scared me at the time, even though it was something I'd always fantasized about. You know how it goes. I was twenty-two, been in school since I was five, thought I was ready to get on with my life…. I won't say Gretchen and I were deliriously happy, but we got along well enough during the three years we were married. Until she ran off with the dentist, of course," he finished with a grimace.

Mia had met him not long after that humiliation, when he was still stinging from his wife's betrayal. She'd never met Gretchen, but from the few things he had told her, she doubted that she would have liked her very much, even though Connor had been very careful not to say anything too derogatory about his ex.

"Sounds like Gretchen had a little more in common with Brandy than you'd realized," she murmured.

He winced and pushed a hand through his already-messy sandy hair. "Maybe I just have a knack for picking the wrong women."

"You still haven't told me why you think you have to quit medical school. Or what the lawyer told you that upset you so badly."

The way his jaw tightened let her know that he was deliberately taking his time about that. Whatever it was, she could tell it was major.

"What I didn't know when Brandy left was that she was pregnant," he said after drawing a deep breath. "With my child. Apparently, she didn't want me to know because she didn't want that bond between us."

"You have a child?" Mia asked, her eyes going wide.

He nodded, looking dazed again. "A little girl. She's six years old. Her name is Alexis."

"Oh, my God."

He gave a short laugh that held no humor. "Yeah. That was pretty much my reaction."

"And you never knew anything about this?"

"Nothing. I haven't heard a word from Brandy since she took off, leaving me a note saying it had been fun, but she was ready for some new adventures."

"And now she wants you to be a father to her child?" Becoming incensed on his behalf, Mia let go of his hands to clench her own into fists. "What does she want? Money?"

He shook his head. "No. It's not that."

"Then what?"

"Brandy didn't raise Alexis. She gave the baby to her mother in Springfield, Missouri, to raise, and then she took off again. A year ago, she was killed in some sort of accident in New Zealand."

"She's—"

"She's dead," he reiterated bluntly. "And as of two days ago, so is her mother. A massive heart attack. Which is why the lawyer contacted me."

Connor watched Mia's face as the realization dawned on her. "They want you to take the little girl?"

Still finding it hard to believe himself, he nodded. "Alexis has only one surviving maternal family member. An aunt, Brandy's older sister. The aunt doesn't want to raise the child. She thought I should be notified before she turned Alexis over as a ward of the state."

"Oh." Relaxing the fists she'd clenched, Mia twisted her fingers in her lap. "So they knew about you."

"Brandy gave them my name. In case anything ever happened to her, she said, or in case her daughter ever wanted to know who her father was."

"Do you think there's any chance she lied? That you aren't the father?"

"There will be paternity tests, of course, but Brandy was not a liar. She was almost ruthlessly honest about everything. Apparently, I'm even named as the father on the birth certificate."

"So you believe Alexis is your daughter."

She seemed to be trying to convince herself. He nodded, anyway. "If Brandy said she is, then I don't seem to have any other choice. The lawyer—his name was Haskell. Art Haskell, I think. Anyway, he said it's up to me what I want to do now, but I need to make a decision quickly. Brandy's sister is giving me until Monday to decide whether to accept custody or to relinquish my parental rights so Alexis can be adopted by someone else."

"But you've already made up your mind."

He wasn't surprised by her insight. Mia probably knew him better than anyone else in the world. "I have no other choice," he said again. "She's my daughter, Mia. I can't just turn my back on her."

His daughter. The words felt alien on his tongue. Somewhere in Missouri was a six-year-old child with his DNA. He reached into his pocket and withdrew a photograph Haskell had given him. "This is Alexis."

He noted that Mia's hand wasn't quite steady when she took it. He could certainly understand that.

She studied the picture for several long minutes, then looked up at him somberly. "She looks just like you."

He'd seen the resemblance immediately. Alexis looked like a feminized version of himself at the same age, down to the little dimple in her chin. "I know."

"She really is your daughter."

"I know."

Handing the photo back to him, she shook her head as if to clear it. "Okay, I understand why you feel an obligation to her. But are you sure you want to take responsibility for this child you've never met and who has never met you? That's an enormous undertaking."

"Tell me about it," he muttered. "At least most single dads have the advantage of being in the kid's life from the beginning. I don't know how she's going to react to me. But what else can I do, Mia? Turn her over to the state? Would you be able to do that if it were your child?"

She hesitated a moment, then shook her head. "Of course not. Nor would I expect you to. That's just not who you are. It's not going to be easy, Connor, but you know that."

"Yeah. I know."

"Still, I can't bear the thought of your quitting medical school. Not now."

"I hate it, too," he admitted glumly. "But what else can I do? You've seen how much of a time commitment it requires. There's just no way I can handle that and raise a kid by myself."

"Isn't there anyone else who can help you? Someone from your family?"

"If my mom were still around, she'd be thrilled to help. She always wanted grandkids," he said, sadness gripping his heart. But his mother had died of cancer. He still missed her every day.

"My only surviving grandmother lives in Nebraska and is in poor health, so she's not an option. My dad is a great guy, but he'd be no help. He's been a traveling salesman my whole life. Still travels a great deal. His concept of fatherhood was to play with me when he was home on weekends. The day-to-day practicalities of parenthood were all on my mom's shoulders. He'll spoil Alexis rotten when he meets her, I imagine, but as for being any real help…"

He shook his head. "I can't afford to hire a full-time nanny, so that won't work, either. Alexis will be in school during the day, but there are still evenings and weekends and holidays to deal with—hours I would have to spend studying to finish med school without flunking out. I just can't—"

"I'll help you."

She had spoken quickly, as if on a sudden impulse, but her expression looked certain.

He frowned. "How could you?"

"I could move in with you," she said, taking him completely by surprise again.

"Platonically, of course," she added, as if there were any doubt. "My job is ideal for raising kids. I work during her school hours. We'd only need child care for a couple of hours a day and you could manage that financially. Evenings and weekends, I'll take care of her while you study. I'll do the cooking, the housekeeping, the laundry. I don't have a lot of experience with young children, but I've got nieces and nephews around that age. I'm sure I can manage."

"Why would you even consider this?" he asked, genuinely bewildered by the magnitude of her offer.

She shrugged and he could almost see her mind working. "It could actually be beneficial for both of us. You know I've been saving money to start graduate school after teaching for another year or two. Not having to pay the lease on this apartment would go a long way toward those savings. Your place is paid for, and I'd trade child care for rent there. I'd help you with some expenses, of course, but it would still save me several hundred dollars a month to share your house."

It sounded to him as though she were trying to rationalize her impetuous offer. "It's too much, Mia. I couldn't ask—"

"You didn't ask," she broke in to remind him. "I offered. Think about it. This could be a win-win situation for both of us. I've even thought about taking an evening job in a bookstore or something to earn a little extra for my grad school expenses. This would save my having to do that."

"Mia…"

"Connor." She rested her hands on his again, her eyes locking with his. "You are one of the best friends I've ever had. You're a good, decent man who'll make a wonderful doctor. The world needs doctors like you. It would break my heart if you had to walk away from that dream now because of a youthful indiscretion. Wouldn't you do the same to help me achieve my dreams?"

He wanted to believe he would do anything for Mia. She was such a good friend. Such a good person. Of course he wanted her to be happy. But what she offered was so overwhelming. So life-changing. Would he really be that unselfish?

"Why don't you think about it tonight?" she suggested, seeing the conflicting emotions on his face. "Don't do anything rash without at least considering what I've suggested, will you? I think we can do this, Connor. I think we can work together to provide a home for Alexis while you finish medical school and while I work toward my own educational goals."

"I'll think about it," he agreed slowly. "But you need to do the same. You made an impulsive offer because you care about me, but you need to really consider what would be involved if you do this. Like you said, we don't know this child. We don't know what kind of raising she's had, whether she's been expected to follow rules or have respect for other people and their property. She could be a holy terror, for all we know. And you're talking about spending every evening and weekend with her—what would that do to your social life?"

She laughed. "You, of all people, should know that I don't have that much of a social life to worry about. I'm hardly a party girl."

"What about the guy you went out with last night?"

She shuddered, giving the gesture an extra touch of drama for emphasis. "If I never see that jerk again, I'll be quite happy, thank you. If I'd had to move his hand off my bottom one more time, I might have gone ballistic. As it was, his life was hanging by a very thin thread. I gave Natalie a piece of my mind later for setting me up with such a creep, but she swore she didn't know he was that bad."

The thought of some guy putting those moves on Mia made Connor's blood boil. He told himself he'd have been as defensive on behalf of any of his women friends, and then tried to believe it. "You should have broken his fingers."

"I considered it. I think he finally realized I was edging toward violence. He looked a little nervous toward the end of the evening."

Her light tone invited him to laugh with her, but he couldn't seem to tap into his sense of humor tonight. "It's getting late," he said. "I'd better go. Like you said, we both need to think about this."

"I know my offer was spur of the moment, but I won't change my mind. The more I think about it, the more I know it's the right thing to do. It's the only solution to your problem, and not such a bad deal for me, either."

She'd obviously convinced herself. He was going to need a little more time to process. He'd had too much thrown at him today.

But there was certainly some appeal to the idea of Mia sharing his home. As a friend, of course, he assured himself as he left her apartment a few minutes later. A temporary solution to a very big dilemma.

Maybe it wouldn't hurt to give her plan a try.

Mia shook her head when Connor looked at his watch for what had to be the dozenth time in the past ten minutes. "Constantly checking won't make the time pass any more quickly," she reminded him.

Looking sheepish, he dropped his arm. "I know. I'm just…antsy," he admitted.

As if that was something she didn't already know.

It was Tuesday afternoon, and the minutes were creeping toward 5 p.m., the time when Patricia Caple, Alexis's aunt, had said she would arrive at Connor's house with the girl.

Connor had offered to drive to Springfield to fetch the child, but Patricia had refused. Mia suspected she didn't want Connor to know where she lived, for some reason. Maybe so he couldn't return Alexis if he changed his mind about keeping her?

As if a child were a sweater or something that could be returned if the fit wasn't perfect, she thought in exasperation.

Connor was a nervous wreck and she couldn't say she blamed him. She could not imagine how it must feel for him to be on the verge of meeting the daughter he hadn't known existed for six years.

She was more than a little anxious herself.

As she had promised him, she had not changed her mind about her reckless offer during the three days that had passed since she'd made it. Even though her parents had expressed concerns about her decision. Even though Natalie had asked her flatly if she had lost her mind. Even though she knew the gossips would have a field day with her moving in with Connor, despite her stated reasons for doing so. Even though she was occasionally overwhelmed with the reality of what she was doing, of how much responsibility she was taking on.

Just don't let me mess this up, she prayed silently as she had quite a few times during the past few days. She hoped she was up to the challenge she had given herself.

The doorbell finally rang at 5:05 p.m. Stopping mid-pace, Connor took a moment to smooth his hair before moving toward the door, a gesture Mia found touching. He wanted to look nice when his daughter saw him for the first time. He was clean-shaven and dressed in a nice green shirt and neatly pressed khakis.

She, too, had freshened up after work, brushing her shoulder-length brown hair into a shiny curtain and donning a fresh pink top and gray slacks. Curious, she moved to stand behind him as he opened the door.

Patricia Caple was a tall, thin, bleached blonde with full breasts pushed upward into a black, scoop-necked sweater. Her high-heeled boots looked very expensive, as did her diamond earrings and the rings that glittered on her hands. It didn't look to Mia as if money was her reason for declining to raise her niece.

"You're Connor Hayes?" Patricia asked, giving him a long once-over.

He nodded, his gaze already going to the child half-hidden behind Patricia's left leg. "Yes. You must be Patricia."

Mia knew he'd already spoken to the woman by phone a couple of times and had expressed his sympathy at the loss of her mother and her sister. He'd told Mia afterward that whatever Patricia felt about those losses, she hadn't shared her feelings with him. From what she saw now, Mia suspected Patricia kept her emotions locked tightly inside her carefully smoothed and perfectly made-up face.

"Yes. And this is Alexis. Say hello to your daddy, Lex."

Patricia pulled the little girl forward as she spoke, and Mia was struck by her first sight of the child. She was a beauty. Her hair was still childhood-blond, although it looked as if it would darken with age. Her eyes, like Connor's, were large and very dark blue, framed in long, dark lashes. Her little face was flushed, and the dimpled chin a bit unsteady when she gazed up at the father she didn't know.

"Hello," she whispered, obeying her aunt's instructions.

Connor's voice was husky when he responded. "Hello, Alexis. I'm very glad to meet you."

She didn't respond as she continued to look at him with searching eyes.

"This is Mia Doyle," he said, including both the child and her aunt in the introduction. "My very good friend."

Patricia gave Mia the same comprehensive assessment with which she'd greeted Connor. "You're the nanny?"

"In a manner of speaking," Mia agreed, knowing Connor had given the woman a brief explanation of the arrangements he'd made for his child's care.

"She's a good kid," Patricia said somewhat off-handedly. "My mother raised her right. I guess she learned from the mistakes she made with Brandy."

Mia didn't know what to say to that.

Patricia turned toward her car. "I'll get her bags."

"Let me help you," Connor said, moving forward. "Alexis, you can stay here and get to know Mia, okay?"

The child nodded, her somber eyes focused on Mia now. Mia held out a hand to the little girl. "Come into the living room, Alexis. We can get comfortable."

Once again, the child obeyed without protest, sliding one cold little hand into Mia's. Only then did Mia notice the somewhat grubby stuffed cat clutched in a death grip in Alexis's other arm. "What's your cat's name?"

"Pete," Alexis said quietly. "My mama gave him to me when I was little."

"Did she?" She wondered how much contact Alexis had

actually had with her mother. Or did she refer to the grandmother who had raised her? "I like the name Pete."

Alexis nodded, her fine hair swaying around her face. "Me, too."

"Are you hungry? I'm making spaghetti for dinner."

"I'm a little hungry. And I like spaghetti."

Most children did, which was why Mia had chosen to make that particular dish that evening. She'd made brownies for dessert, another popular treat for her nieces and nephews.

"We'll eat soon," she promised, sitting on the couch and drawing Alexis down beside her. "I'm sure you must be tired after your long drive. Did you have a good trip?"

"Aunt Patricia plays the radio kind of loud. But we had hamburgers."

Mia suspected that Patricia had played the radio as an excuse to avoid making conversation with a six-year-old for four hours. Patricia didn't seem antagonistic or particularly unkind toward Alexis; it was more that she seemed detached. Almost indifferent.

"I like an occasional hamburger myself," she assured the child.

Connor and Patricia returned then, each carrying one bag that presumably contained the child's clothes. Connor had a pink backpack in his other hand, and Patricia bore a bag that might have held toys. It wasn't a lot of stuff considering it was everything the little girl owned.

"Okay," Patricia said, both physically and metaphorically brushing off her hands after setting down her load. "I guess I'll be on my way."

"You're not driving back to Springfield tonight, are you?" Connor asked with a frown. "You're welcome to stay here. I'm sure we can make room."

"Thank you, but no. I have plans tomorrow." She held out a hand to him. "Goodbye, Connor. It was nice to finally meet you."

Giving her hand a quick shake, he replied courteously, "It

was nice to meet you, too. If you're ever in the neighborhood, feel free to—"

"Thank you," she said, already turning toward Mia.

They shook hands briefly, murmuring platitudes.

Patricia looked down at Alexis then, and for just a moment, Mia thought she might have seen a glimmer of emotion in the woman's eyes. She couldn't interpret what she'd seen, but she thought it might have been just a hint of regret. Sorrow, perhaps?

"You be good for your daddy and Ms. Doyle," she instructed, no emotion in her voice.

The child nodded and said quietly, "Yes, ma'am."

Patricia leaned over to give her a quick, careful hug. "Goodbye, Lex."

"'Bye, Aunt Tricia."

Patricia turned without another look at any of them and let herself out of the house. Her posture made it clear that she didn't want any of them to try and detain her.

Mia and Connor shared a quizzical look over Alexis's head. And then Connor swallowed visibly and turned to his daughter.

To bring himself closer to her eye level, he sat on the edge of a chair, his forearms resting on his thighs. "So your aunt told you that I'm your father."

The child nodded. "You knew my mama before I was born."

"Do you remember your mama?"

"She used to come visit us in Springfield. She gave me Pete," she added, holding up the stuffed gray cat. "And she told me I would meet my daddy someday."

Connor looked startled. Even though she wasn't a big believer in such things, Mia wondered if Brandy had had some sort of premonition of her untimely death. Or maybe she had intended to contact Connor herself had she lived longer.

"My grandma went to heaven to be with my mama," Alexis added. "Aunt Tricia said they're together now."

His eyes grave, Connor nodded. "Yes, I'm sure they are."

"She said I was going to live with you now. She said I'll like living here."

Her throat tight, Mia watched Connor moisten his lips before replying, "I hope you will. I'm very glad you've come to live with me, Alexis. I'm sorry I haven't seen you before, but I didn't know about you."

"I know. Aunt Tricia told me."

Mia couldn't help wondering about the child's composure, which seemed rather advanced for her years. Had she learned that skill from her aunt? Was she masking the fears and insecurities that would have been only natural under these circumstances? After all, her whole world had just been turned upside down. Yet she seemed to accept her new situation as easily as if she'd just changed clothes.

Mia worried a little that such repression couldn't be good for a little girl. It had been traumatic enough for Connor and her to make these huge changes.

Mia had spent all day yesterday moving into one of the two spare bedrooms in Connor's small frame house. The room had been unfurnished, so he'd helped her carry her own bedroom furniture in. The room was plenty large enough for her queen-size bed, dresser and chest, as well as a small bookcase to hold the books she had wanted to have with her there. There was a nice-size closet for her clothes. She had brought only the necessities for now, stashing her extra furniture and possessions in an inexpensive storage unit close by.

Alexis would sleep in an identical bedroom next door to Mia's. Connor had already furnished that room as a guest room, with a bed, a dresser, a small writing desk and a bookcase, all furniture he said had belonged to his mother. The beddings were a plain navy blue and there were few decorations in the room. It hardly looked like a little girl's room, but they'd agreed that they would remedy that after Alexis arrived, letting her help them decorate the room to her taste. They'd hoped that would make her feel more at home.

The small house had only one bathroom, but it was a nice-size one, and they figured they could come up with a schedule that would make it all work out. The bathroom was located in the back hallway with Connor's room on one end and the two smaller rooms on the other side.

Both of them had braced themselves for a more difficult arrival. Mia had warned Connor that Alexis might cry or try to cling to her aunt when she was dropped off with two strangers. She suspected that Connor was as surprised as she was that the transition had been so easy.

Alexis looked around at Mia. "I'm still a little hungry."

Mia smiled. "I'll put the finishing touches on the spaghetti. Your dad can show you your bedroom."

"Okay."

Connor rose and picked up as many of the bags as he could carry in one trip. "You can bring your backpack, can't you, Alexis?"

"Sure." She slung the strap over her shoulder and followed as he led her out of the living room.

Still concerned that this was all going a bit too easily, Mia watched them leave the room. And then she turned toward the kitchen.

Sipping a glass of iced tea, Connor studied his daughter over the rim of his glass, trying to be surreptitious as he stared at her from across the table.

His daughter. When would those words stop sounding so foreign to him? When would it feel natural to have her here, to know that he was now responsible for everything concerning her?

She was a funny little thing. Maybe she'd spent too much time with adults. She seemed oddly mature for her age, occasionally using big words that sounded strange in her little-girl lisp. She'd been slightly pale when she arrived, and he'd thought he detected a bit of uncertainty in her eyes when she'd first looked up at him, but since then she'd been composed and seemingly satisfied with her new home.

He'd apologized for the lack of color in her bedroom, and she'd looked intrigued when he'd told her that Mia was going to take her shopping for new bedding and decorations. She'd seemed especially pleased that Mia would be sleeping just next door. He'd pointed out his own room to her as well. She'd spared only a glance in that direction.

"There's a backyard you can play in," he'd told her as they headed back to rejoin Mia for dinner. "It's not very big, but it has a fence and a little patio with a table and chairs. There's room for a swing set; I'll get one for you, if you like."

"I like to swing," she had answered agreeably. "I had a swing set at my grandma's house."

"Then you'll have one here," he assured her, hoping he could find a good deal on a set. He could already tell that raising a child was going to be expensive. He'd been studying his finances ever since he'd learned that he would be doing so.

Haskell, the attorney, had informed him that Alexis had been the beneficiary of her grandmother's insurance policy, so there was an account set up in the child's name to help with expenses. Connor had wondered how Patricia had felt about that, but Patricia hadn't seemed to hold any resentment when she'd given him the paperwork outside at the car. The envelope had also held Alexis's birth certificate, Social Security card and immunization records, information he would need to enroll her in school.

The insurance policy had been for a hundred thousand dollars, he'd discovered somewhat to his surprise. That would go a long way in helping him out, but he had made a vow to himself not to touch it unless it became absolutely necessary. That money would be for Alexis's future, for her college education. He could support his own daughter in the meantime—

even if it was on medical school loan money that he would have to repay once he'd finally earned his M.D.

At least he didn't have to worry about paying a mortgage. This house was small and located in an aging, working-class neighborhood, but it belonged to him. It had been a gift from his dad after Connor's mother died. Connor's father, Duncan Hayes, had sold the larger house where he'd lived with his wife for more than thirty years, saying he didn't need a place that big just for himself, especially because he still traveled so much in his job.

Duncan had purchased a tidy condo for himself and had insisted on buying a place for Connor, who'd still been recovering from the expensive divorce. Knowing that Connor had been preparing medical school applications then, Duncan had called the house an inheritance from his late wife, who would be so proud of her son for finally pursuing his dreams. Put that way, Connor had been unable to refuse the generous gift, although he'd worried about whether his dad had put enough aside to fund his retirement. Duncan had brushed those concerns aside, saying his future was taken care of, and now it was time for Connor to concentrate on his own.

Of course, neither of them had known at the time that Connor would soon become fully responsible for someone other than himself.

"How's your spaghetti, Alexis?" Mia asked to keep the conversation moving when Connor found himself with little to say.

"It's good. I like the meatballs."

Mia smiled. "I'm glad. They're my mother's recipe."

"Is your mother in heaven, too?"

"No, sweetie. My mother lives in Hot Springs. That's a little over an hour's drive from here."

"Oh. What about your daddy?" the child asked with a quick glance at Connor.

"He lives there, too. And I have a brother named Paul who lives near them with his wife, Carla. He has two children, an eight-year-old boy named Nicklaus and a nine-year-old girl named Caroline."

"I'd like to meet them sometime."

"I'm sure they would love to meet you, too," Mia assured her. "I'll take you to Hot Springs sometime soon. It's an interesting town."

"Okay."

Connor realized that in the years he'd known Mia, he'd never met any of her family. Now he wondered why that was. Had she deliberately kept her friendship with him separate from her family life? Their mutual friends were all associated with their jobs—well, his former job—as teachers.

He wondered what she had told her family about her current living arrangements. How they had felt about what she'd done. He'd been so caught up in his own problems during the weekend that he hadn't even thought to ask her.

"Tomorrow," Mia said, still talking to Alexis, "I'm taking a day off my job as a teacher, and you and I will work in your room. Your dad has classes to attend in the morning, and then tomorrow afternoon he's going to take you to enroll in school. You'd like to get back into school and start making some new friends, wouldn't you?"

Alexis nodded. "I'm in the first grade. I can read a little. And I'm good at math."

"I can already tell you're a very bright girl," Mia said approvingly.

"My teacher's name was Miss Albertson. She said I was a very good student."

Connor heard a touch of wistfulness in Alexis's voice when she mentioned her teacher. She was probably going to miss her school and her friends there more than she wanted them to know. He hoped she would settle in quickly to her new school, and that she would make new friends there.

Mia looked at him, as though wondering why he'd grown

so quiet and so somber. He forced a smile and tried to think of something worthwhile to contribute. "I'm in school, too, Alexis," he said. "Did your aunt tell you that? I'm studying to become a doctor."

Tilting her head, the child eyed him questioningly. "You're kind of old to be in school," she said after a moment.

He winced. "Well—"

Looking suddenly stricken, she added quickly, "You're not too old, though. Probably everyone's like you in doctor school."

"It's okay," he assured her with a laugh. "You didn't hurt my feelings. It's sort of cool that we're both going to school, isn't it? And Mia's a teacher, so we'll all be at school every day."

Reassured that she hadn't said anything wrong, Alexis relaxed and took another big bite of her spaghetti. Connor concentrated on finishing his own meal. So far, he wasn't exactly proving to be a natural at this. If he could barely carry on a mealtime conversation with the kid, how was he going to handle all the other millions of responsibilities that came with this job?

He thanked his lucky stars that he had Mia to help him.

Chapter Three

Mia helped Alexis unpack her bags after dinner while Connor studied in the living room. The child had brought a functional wardrobe of knits and jeans, plenty of new-looking underwear and socks and two nice dresses that still had price tags dangling. "Did your aunt take you shopping before you came?"

Alexis nodded. "She said I needed some new clothes. She bought me these sneakers, too. And the pretty black shoes for dress up."

"That was nice of her." Mia wondered if Patricia would miss her niece. If it had been at all difficult for her to give her up. It had been so hard to tell what the other woman was thinking.

Alexis unpacked the bag of toys, mostly dolls and accessories. She arranged them neatly on the shelves of the small bookcase, amusingly particular about their placement.

"You like dolls?"

Alexis nodded again. "I like to play school with them. I'm the teacher. That's what I want to be when I grow up. Like you."

"I'm sure you'll be a wonderful teacher."

The child yawned and rubbed her eyes. She'd had a very long day, Mia thought sympathetically. Quite an emotional upheaval as well, although she seemed to be handling it amazingly well. "You must be getting tired after your long day. Would you like to take a bath and put on your pajamas? I can read you a bedtime story, if you like."

"My grandma always read to me." Alexis unzipped her pink backpack and pulled out a handful of children's books. "These are my favorites. We couldn't bring them all because Aunt Tricia said there wasn't room, but she let me bring these."

Mia thought she'd have found a way to transport every one of the little girl's personal possessions, but she kept the opinion to herself. She supposed Patricia had done the best she could for her niece. "Then we'll read one of your favorites tonight."

Half an hour later, Alexis was bathed and dressed in soft pink pajamas. She looked small and fragile with her little bare feet peeking out from beneath the hems of the slightly too-long pajama bottoms, her freshly washed-and-dried, blond-streaked hair waving around her rosy face. Looking at the child, Mia was struck by another wave of self-doubt. She had waded into all this responsibility on a generous impulse. Had she really done the right thing? For Alexis? For herself?

She cleared her throat, reminding herself that it was too late to deal with those issues now. Alexis was here and Mia had volunteered to care for her. This was no time to change her mind.

"Let's go say good night to your daddy," she suggested, "and then I'll read you a story and tuck you in."

"Okay." Clutching Pete in her other arm, Alexis slipped her hand into Mia's.

Wrapping her fingers around the little girl's, Mia led her out of the bedroom.

Connor was immersed in his books in a familiar pose, and Mia hoped he would be able to pull himself out of his studies long enough to say a coherent good night to his daughter. She cleared her throat rather loudly as they entered the room. "Alexis wants to tell you good night."

His hair disheveled, his jaw covered with an evening shadow, his eyes a little unfocused, Connor looked up from his notes. Mia's heart tripped as the pure masculine appeal of him hit her, and she chided herself silently for reacting that way. First Alexis and now Connor had elicited very strong responses from her within the last ten minutes. She needed to settle down and remind herself why she was here.

The nanny, Patricia had called her, and while the term wasn't exactly accurate, it was close enough. She needed to think of herself that way—not a part of this little family, but someone here to help them out.

Connor made a visible effort to concentrate on something other than his studies. "Is there anything you need before you turn in, Alexis?"

"No, thank you. Mia's going to read me a story."

"Yeah? That's nice of her." He gave Mia a quick smile of gratitude before looking at his daughter again. "You let us know if there's anything you need tonight, okay?"

"Okay."

"Good night, Alexis."

"'Night." She didn't add "Daddy." Mia realized the child had yet to refer to Connor by that term. Not so odd, of course. After all, he was still basically a stranger to her.

"Maybe you'd like to give her a good-night kiss?" she prodded, thinking they needed to get past this awkward, reserved stage quickly if Alexis was going to feel safe and secure in her new home.

"Oh, yeah, sure."

Alexis glanced up a bit uncertainly at Mia. Smiling encouragingly down at her, Mia led her to the couch. Connor leaned over to brush a light kiss on Alexis's cheek. "Good night."

"'Night," she said again.

It was a start, Mia figured. With a little nod to Connor, she turned and walked with Alexis out of the room.

Alexis looked even smaller in the big bed with the dark linens around her. They were definitely going to have to lighten things up in here, Mia decided, thinking a shopping trip was in order at the earliest opportunity. "Which book would you like to hear tonight?"

Without even stopping to consider, Alexis replied, "*Green Eggs and Ham.*"

"That sounds good." Mia plucked the book from the stack and stretched out beside the girl. Alexis rested her head trustingly against Mia's arm as she began to read, holding the book so Alexis could see the pictures. She read in a quiet, soothing tone, and Alexis was almost asleep by the time the story ended.

Sliding off the bed, Mia tucked the covers snugly around the child and her treasured stuffed cat. "I'll be sleeping right next door if you need anything tonight," she reminded her. "Just call out or come get me."

"Okay."

"Do you want me to leave the night-light on?" She'd brought the night-light herself, a whimsical little glass unicorn that plugged into an outlet and glowed a soothing blue. It had been a gift from one of her students last year and she'd thought a child would appreciate the soft illumination in a strange place.

"Yes, please. And could you leave the door open so you can hear me if I call you?"

"Of course I will." Leaning over the bed, Mia pressed a kiss to Alexis's cheek. "Good night, sweetie."

Alexis surprised her by wrapping her arms around her neck and giving her a quick hug. "Good night, Mia."

Touched, Mia straightened and tucked the covers in again. After hesitating only a moment, she turned and left the room, leaving the door an inch ajar, just as Alexis had requested.

* * *

Connor wasn't on the couch when Mia walked into the living room. Looking around for him, she found him standing at the window, staring out into the night. Judging from his expression, she doubted that he saw a thing beyond the glass. He seemed to be lost in his thoughts, and they were apparently somber ones.

"Connor?"

He hadn't heard her come in, which was only further indication of how distracted he'd been. He turned quickly. "Oh. Mia."

She smiled. "You were expecting someone else?"

"No, I just…" He pushed a hand through his hair. "Did you get her tucked in okay?"

"Yes. She was so tired, I think she'll sleep soundly."

"I hope so."

"Are you okay? Do you need anything?"

He started to shake his head, then stopped himself and raised his hands in a gesture of bewilderment. "I don't know if I can do this."

She knew exactly what he was going through now. And because she did, she placed a hand on his forearm and smiled encouragingly up at him. "I understand. It's terrifying, isn't it?"

He covered her hand with his and his fingers felt cold. "That's exactly what it is."

"She's a sweet little girl, Connor. Very well-behaved."

"Yeah, I know. I can't help but wonder if she's a little too well-behaved. Did that seem normal to you?"

She shook her head in exasperation. "First you were worried that she would be a terror and now you're worried that she's too good?"

"I know, it seems crazy," he admitted. "But I just got the feeling that she's repressing a lot."

"Of course she is. How could she not be with all that's happened to her lately?"

"Maybe she needs to be in counseling or something. I mean, I'm certainly no expert on kids and grief. I don't have the slightest clue what I should be doing with her."

"I'm no expert either, but I know that children need love and acceptance. You can give her that."

"Can I?" His eyes looked tortured. "I don't even know what I feel right now. I look at her and I think, this is my daughter. My little girl. And yet I don't know her. I don't know her favorite foods, or colors, or what she's thinking when she looks back at me so seriously."

"Those things will come with time, for both of you. She doesn't know you either," she reminded him. "But she seems willing to give you a chance."

"She needs someone who can spend time with her. Who really has the time to get to know her. Someone who isn't studying sixteen hours a day and worrying about studying the other eight hours."

"That's why I'm here. When you're busy, I'll take care of her. I'll help you get to know her."

His fingers tightened over hers. "I don't know how to thank you for what you're doing. I honestly don't know what I would have done without you."

She shrugged a little. "You'd have managed."

But probably not without quitting medical school, she thought. Not without giving up his dream. How could she not do everything she could to prevent that? She loved him—as a dear friend, of course. She wanted him to have it all. Didn't everyone want that for their closest friends? She was sure he felt the same way about her, even if there hadn't been an occasion for him to prove it the way she was for him.

He searched her face. "This doesn't scare you at all?"

Her laugh was shakier than she would have liked. "Come on, you know me better than that. I had a moment of panic in her bedroom. I came very close to bolting and telling you

you're on your own, pal. She just looked so darned vulnerable and tiny."

For some reason, her confession actually seemed to help him relax a little. Maybe he'd just needed to know that his fears were reasonable. "Yeah. Exactly."

"We can do this, Connor," she said, pulling her hand away with a last bracing pat to his arm. "You're going to be a good father to her, and I'll figure out how to be a nanny until she's all settled in. By the time I'm ready to start grad school, you and she will be very comfortable with each other, and she'll have a ton of new friends at school and she'll be old enough to leave with a part-time caretaker after school and on weekends. You aren't the only single parent in medical school, I bet. Somehow or other, it will work out."

She wasn't sure why she'd felt the need to remind him—maybe both of them—that this arrangement was only temporary. He frowned for a moment, then moistened his lips and nodded. "Yeah. I guess you're right. Thanks for the pep talk."

"Any time. Now, why don't I make you some hot tea? It'll help you relax while you get back to your studying."

He leaned over to brush his lips across her cheek, much the same way he had with Alexis. "Thanks, Mia. That sounds great."

Resisting an impulse to press her hand to the spot his lips had touched, she nodded and moved toward the kitchen without saying anything more.

Something woke Mia in the middle of the night. She opened her eyes and squinted into the darkness, trying to decide what it had been. Was she still adjusting to her new surroundings? Hearing the creaks of an unfamiliar house? Or had there been something else?

Hearing a sound again, she slid her feet out of the bed. She thought it had come from Alexis's room.

Without bothering to don a robe over her brushed satin

pajamas, she walked barefoot through her door and into the hallway. She pushed open the door to Alexis's room quietly and peeked inside, trying to identify the sound that had awakened her. Was the child having a bad dream? That would certainly be understandable.

The sound came again, and she recognized it this time with a pang through her heart. Alexis was crying softly into her pillow.

"Oh, baby, it's okay," she said, hurrying across the room to gather the little girl into her arms. "Everything's going to be all right, I promise."

Alexis burrowed into Mia's arms, tucking her head tightly beneath Mia's chin. "I'm sorry," she whispered.

"No, don't be sorry. It's okay to cry when you need to."

Sniffling, Alexis murmured, "Aunt Tricia didn't like it when I cried. She said it made her sad."

"It's okay to be sad sometimes," Mia replied, instinctively rocking the child against her. "Especially when you've lost someone you loved. I cry when I'm sad, too."

Her breath catching, Alexis pulled back just a little, her tear-streaked face just visible in the bluish night light. "You do?"

"Of course I do." Mia brushed a damp strand of hair away from the little girl's mouth. "And when I'm feeling scared and lonely, I lean on my friends. I'm your friend, Alexis. You can lean on me tonight, okay?"

Alexis snuggled against her again, her sobs quieting. "I miss my grandma."

"I know you do, baby. I'm sorry."

"Does he want me here?"

The non sequitur confused her for a moment, but then she rested her head on Alexis's soft hair and murmured, "Of course your daddy wants you here, honey. He's just a little nervous. Like you are. He wants you to like him and he wants to be a good daddy to you."

Alexis lifted her head again. "He's nervous?"

"Oh, yes. This is all new to him, too. But he's very glad you're here, Alexis."

A sound came from the doorway. Connor stood silhouetted by the hall light behind him. "I heard talking. Is everything okay in here?"

Looking over Alexis's head, Mia replied lightly, "Yes, we're fine. Alexis is just getting accustomed to her new bedroom."

"Oh." Although she couldn't see his expression very well in the shadows, she could tell that he felt uncertain of what he should do now. A little left out, perhaps, because Mia seemed to be handling everything without him? "Can I get you anything, Alexis?" he asked.

"No, thank you." Even though still a bit thick from her tears, the child's voice was steady. "I'm sorry I woke you up."

"I wasn't asleep. Y'all let me know if you need anything from me, okay?"

Mia answered for them both. "We will. Good night."

"Um, good night." Slowly, he turned away, pulling the door almost closed behind him to give them privacy.

"Will you stay with me for a little while?" Alexis asked in a whisper.

"Of course I will. I'll lie right here until you go to sleep."

They nestled into the pillows together. Mia lay awake, staring at the ceiling and worrying, long after Alexis drifted off to sleep.

A substitute teacher filled in for Mia on Tuesday so that she could stay with Alexis while Connor attended lectures that morning. She and Connor had arranged for her to pick him up at the medical school campus at 1 p.m. From there, they would have lunch and then go together to register Alexis in school. He had already called a private elementary school near his house and made an appointment with the registrar for 2:30 p.m.

He could have enrolled her in public school, of course, but this one was much more convenient location-wise and had an excellent reputation. The tuition was affordable, barely, he'd admitted to Mia. He would be dipping into his loan money to pay it, but he figured it was worth the expense to have her so close by. The school also provided after-hours care until Mia was able to pick up Alexis every afternoon, which made it an even more appealing choice.

With so much extra time that morning, Mia decided it was as good an opportunity as any to do some shopping. She fastened Alexis into the backseat of her little car and took her to a shopping center near Connor's house in midtown Little Rock, only a few miles from the medical school campus. Holding hands, they entered a reasonably priced home furnishings store in search of bedding suited to a little girl. Less than an hour later, they walked out again carrying full shopping bags.

Alexis appeared delighted with the pastel pink, yellow, mint and lavender striped comforter Mia had found on a clearance rack. Mia was pleased with the price, a full sixty percent off retail. She'd had enough of the money Connor had given her left over to buy two sets of pastel sheets, also on sale, and a couple of throw pillows in coordinating solids, one round, the other heart-shaped. Instead of heavy curtains, she'd bought pink sheers.

As her own contribution to the cause, she'd bought a lamp with a lavender porcelain bottom and a shade with pastel polka dots that matched the colors in the comforter. By the time they arranged Alexis's toys around the room and hung a few framed posters on the walls, the room would be perfect for a six-year-old girl, she decided in satisfaction.

"I like my stuff," Alexis said as Mia fastened her into the car again. "My room is going to be pretty."

"Yes, it will be. Just like you."

Alexis giggled, her mood dramatically different from her sadness during the night.

Connor waited at the corner where they'd agreed to meet.

He climbed into the passenger seat, tossing the backpack that held his textbooks and laptop computer into the backseat next to Alexis. "What have you ladies been up to this morning? Did you get your shopping done?"

Alexis nodded, a bit shy now that he'd joined them, but still smiling. "I got a new comforter. It's pink and purple and green and yellow, and it's beautiful. It's in the trunk."

"I can't wait to see it," he assured her, giving Mia a look that expressed his pleasure with Alexis's good mood.

She smiled back at him. "You'll be even happier when you see the receipt," she assured him. "We found bargains."

"Just what a guy likes to hear."

They had lunch at a deli, where Mia and Connor ordered sandwiches and Alexis had a bowl of chicken noodle soup. The server forgot to bring crackers to go with the soup, and she made a second trip to bring them with an apology. "Is there anything else you need?" she asked Alexis.

"No, thank you."

The server smiled at Mia and Connor. "You have a very polite little girl," she said, including them both in the compliment. "Cute as a button, too."

Connor murmured a thank you.

Mia supposed she should get used to people thinking they were a family. It would happen whenever she went out in public with Connor and Alexis. Because there was no need to correct strangers, she should simply learn to take such comments in stride.

It still felt funny to hear it, though.

They arrived at the school a few minutes early, which gave them time to look around a little from the car. The grounds were tidy and well-groomed, with a large playground filled with play equipment. The children they saw wore uniforms: khaki pants and navy, red or white polo shirts for the boys; khaki pants or skirts or a navy-and-red plaid jumper with navy, red or white polo shirts for the girls.

"It looks like a nice place," Mia said to Alexis, half turning to study the child's expression.

"Why are they all dressed alike?" Alexis asked, craning to see the children on the playground. She had already unbuckled her seat belt and she knelt on the backseat, her hands propped beside Mia as she leaned forward to peer out the windshield.

"They wear school uniforms here. Everyone dresses alike to show that they go to the same school."

"We didn't wear uniforms at my school in Springfield."

"You'll get used to it. Even most of the public schools around this area require uniforms. It just makes things easier for the parents and the students because they don't have to worry about what clothes to choose every day."

"Oh. Okay. Can I get a red bow for my hair like that girl has?"

"Absolutely."

Connor had been riffling though the paperwork he'd brought with him, double checking to see that he had everything he needed. As if a sudden thought had occurred to him, he lifted his head and looked at Mia and then Alexis. "I just realized… What name did you use at your school in Springfield?"

The child looked a bit confused. "Alexis. My friend Madison called me Lexi."

"No, honey, I meant your last name. Your aunt said you use your mom's last name, Caple, but your birth certificate says Alexis Marie Hayes, which is the same last name as mine."

Mia tried not to frown. Brandy certainly hadn't made things easier for her daughter. Why on earth hadn't the woman just told Connor he had a child? But because she felt a little guilty being critical of his late ex-girlfriend, she suppressed the thought without comment.

Alexis shrugged. "My grandma did all the papers at my school there. I don't know what she wrote down."

"What last name did you write on your schoolwork, sweetie?" Mia asked, trying to clarify things for her.

"Caple. The same as my grandma."

Seeing that Connor was biting his lip, as if trying to decide how to handle this, Mia spoke again, "Would you mind very much if you use Alexis Hayes here? I know it will seem strange to you at first, but it would make things much easier for your daddy. For you, too, in the long run."

"Alexis Hayes?" Tilting her head, the child wore a look of concentration as she repeated the name beneath her breath a couple of times. "Okay," she said after a moment. "But I might forget sometimes," she added, looking a bit worried.

Mia reached over to squeeze her hand reassuringly. "You probably will. But that's okay. I'll help you practice writing it when we get home."

"Alexis Hayes," Alexis repeated again, as if committing the name to memory. She glanced sideways at Connor. "It's a nice name."

He smiled at her, looking relieved that the issue had been settled so easily. "Yes. It is. Shall we go in now? It's almost time for our appointment."

Just under twenty minutes later, Alexis Marie Hayes was an official first grader at Sunshine Academy. Connor signed the necessary paperwork authorizing Mia to pick up Alexis at school and to be given full access to her information. Mia would be allowed to talk to the administration and the teachers on Alexis's behalf, just as Connor would, and her name and number were entered as emergency contact information beneath his own.

The principal, a kind-eyed, brusque-voiced woman named Mrs. Montgomery, personally took them on a tour, chatting easily the entire time. She told them about the parent-teacher organization that she was quite sure both Connor and Mia would want to join, and the monthly assemblies at which students were recognized with rewards for good grades and good behavior. She showed them the pristine cafeteria with its colorful muraled walls, and the media center filled with books and computers and whimsical mobiles dangling from the ceiling.

"This will be your classroom, Alexis," she said, stopping at a door with a glass pane through which they could see a young woman standing in front of about twenty students at desks. "Your teacher's name is Miss Chen, and I think you're going to like her a lot. Everyone does."

Tapping on the door, she ushered them in and introduced them to Amy Chen, who looked to be barely out of her teens, but was probably in her mid-twenties, only a year or two younger than Mia. The teacher welcomed Alexis with the now-predictable enthusiasm, then introduced her to the class, who said in unison when prompted, "Hi, Alexis."

"Alexis will see you in the morning," Mrs. Montgomery announced. "I'm sure you'll all be nice enough to make her feel right at home."

"She can sit by me," a little girl with red-orange pigtails tied with white ribbons said, motioning eagerly to the empty desk beside her. "My name's McKenzie."

"All right, McKenzie, we'll all get to know each other tomorrow," her teacher instructed, smiling wryly.

"McKenzie will take your daughter under her wing," she added in an undertone to Mia and Connor. "She's the most outgoing student I have. And by outgoing, I mean talkative," she added with a laugh.

Deciding to correct the teacher later about her relationship to Alexis, Mia only smiled as the principal led them out of the room again.

Later that afternoon, Connor helped Mia and Alexis carry shopping bags into Alexis's bedroom. Some of the bags held the school uniforms they'd stopped to buy on the way home.

Mia and Alexis had selected enough of the mix-and-match pieces to make up several outfits. Enough, Mia had assured him, to last for most of the school year.

Both he and his credit card were happy to hear that.

He duly admired the bedding and accessories they showed him, telling them they'd made very nice choices.

Mia looked at the new decor items and then critically at the off-white walls. "Would you mind if I paint in here?" she asked him.

"Oh, yeah. Sure." All the walls in his house were painted the same off-white they'd been when he bought the place. Although the neutral color had been fine with him, he supposed a child would prefer a brighter color.

Mia nodded in satisfaction. "A soft yellow would be nice in here, don't you think, Alexis?"

"That sounds pretty," Alexis agreed eagerly.

"I'm not sure when I'd have time to paint…"

Mia shook her head. "We wouldn't need your help," she assured him. "I've painted rooms before. It's not that difficult."

"I can help," Alexis volunteered.

Mia smiled at her. "Absolutely. We girls can handle this, can't we?"

Alexis dimpled up at her. "Absolutely," she repeated adorably.

Looking at them grinning at each other, Connor was aware of an odd pang inside him. They seemed to be bonding very quickly. Alexis was obviously taken with Mia, and the feeling was apparently mutual.

Was he feeling a bit excluded? Maybe a little envious that this seemed to be coming so easily to Mia? If so, he should get over it, he told himself firmly. He should be extremely grateful instead that the arrangement they'd made seemed to be getting off to a good start. And he was grateful, of course. It was just…

Just nothing, he thought with a slight shake of his head. Everything was fine.

"So, if you two have everything under control here," he said lightly, "I think I'll join my study group for a few hours. I'm getting behind on my lecture notes."

Mia waved a hand in a gesture of teasing dismissal. "Go. We'll be fine. If you're not home in time for dinner, I'll keep a plate warm for you. Or you can call if you eat with your group."

"I will. Thanks."

He hesitated a moment longer. Should he kiss Alexis goodbye? Was he supposed to do that whenever he left? Did she even want him to?

Mia touched the child's shoulder. "Why don't you give your daddy a hug and thank him for all your new things?" she suggested in a murmur he could just hear.

Her expression shy again, Alexis approached him. "Thank you for all my new things," she recited dutifully.

She still seemed to be avoiding calling him anything. He supposed that would come with time.

Leaning down, he gave her a quick hug. "You're welcome, honey. I'll see you later, okay?"

"Okay." She was already turning back to Mia.

He looked that way himself. When the thought crossed his mind that he wouldn't mind giving Mia a goodbye hug—or even better, a goodbye kiss—he decided it was definitely time for him to go. All this family stuff must be going to his head.

"See you," he said to both of them, and turned a bit more quickly than necessary to make his escape.

Chapter Four

"Where have you been lately, Connor? We've all been worried about you."

Connor responded to Haley's question with a faint smile. "I've been pretty busy the past few days. My, uh, my daughter moved in with me yesterday. I needed to get things in order for her."

His words were met with a moment of startled silence, as he had expected. The other four members of his study group looked at each other, then back at him. Again, it was Haley who spoke. "Did you say your daughter?"

He nodded. "Alexis. She's six."

"And she's living with you now?"

"Yeah."

"Dude," Ron drawled, shaking his head slowly, "how are you going to handle that? I mean, I even had to give my dog to my brother because I didn't have time to care of him."

"Ron," Haley chided him in a stage whisper. "A child is not a dog."

Something about that struck Ron as funny. He started to laugh, but muffled it quickly when Haley gave him another fierce look.

Ignoring their habitual bickering, Anne searched Connor's face with a frown. "I didn't know you had a daughter. You've never mentioned her."

He gave an awkward laugh, wondering exactly how much he should share. "I didn't know I had a daughter either," he said after a moment. "Her mother and I split up before she was born. Her mother died recently and left Alexis for me to raise."

"Wow." Haley shook her head in amazement. "You must be feeling gobsmacked."

"That's one way of putting it."

Hosting again that day, James waved everyone to the table. "I just offered everyone coffee, but maybe you'd rather have a beer?" he asked Connor. "A double bourbon?"

Laughing more naturally now, Connor shook his head. "Thanks, but coffee will be fine."

He piled his books and computer at his usual place at the table, which was already cluttered with everyone else's study materials. And then he reached into the pocket of his jacket and pulled out the photo of Alexis. Weren't dads supposed to share pictures of their kids? "This is my daughter."

Haley snatched the photo out of his fingers. "Oh, she's adorable. Look at that dimple in her chin. Connor, she looks just like you."

Anne took the picture next. "She is pretty. Is she as sweet-natured as she looks?"

"She really is," he admitted in near bemusement. "You'd be amazed at how easily she's adapted to all of this."

Ron studied the picture in turn. "Funny. She does look like you. But on her, it looks good."

Connor chuckled. "Thanks a lot."

Setting cups of coffee on the table, James glanced at the photo. "Cute kid. Where is she now?"

Slipping the photo back into his pocket, Connor took his seat, as did the others, and picked up his coffee cup. "You remember me mentioning my friend, Mia?"

"The schoolteacher who helps you study sometimes?"

He nodded. "She moved in with us. She's going to take care of Alexis while I'm studying."

Ron grinned. "Always suspected there was more between you and Mia than you admitted. Something about the way you talked about her."

Connor shook his head. "No, it's not like that. She has her own room. She's—well, she's sort of a nanny for Alexis for the next year or so. Until Alexis is well settled in and I can make other arrangements. I think it's going to work out fine. Alexis seems to be bonding with Mia very quickly."

Anne frowned. "Won't that be a problem when Mia moves out? I mean, if Alexis becomes too close to her?"

He didn't want to think that far ahead just now. It was all he could do to make it through a day at a time. "We'll deal with that when it comes. Besides, Mia and I are very close friends. She'll always be a part of my life, and Alexis's, too, now."

"Hmm. You've never tried living together before, right?" James asked a bit cynically.

"Well, no. But we've known each other for three years. We've spent a lot of time together."

James shook his dark head, his eyes world-weary, older than his years. "Not the same. Trust me."

Connor thought uncomfortably of his broken marriage. Gretchen had become bored with the habits and routines they had fallen into after the honeymoon phase ended. Everything he did had seemed to annoy her toward the end, and they'd spent more and more time arguing or not speaking at all. Later he had wondered if her affair with her boss had been the cause of her dissatisfaction with him or the result, but whatever the reason, they'd clearly been unsuited.

He would hate to think that he and Mia would ever end up like that, resenting each other, avoiding each other's company, impatient to be free of each other. Was James right? Had he and Mia made a mistake agreeing to spend so much time together?

"So, you're a dad now." Ron studied him thoughtfully. "How weird does that feel?"

"Very," he admitted.

"The dad of a pretty little girl, no less. You'll have boys sniffing around in six or seven years."

He scowled. "She's only six."

"Have you seen how fast girls grow up these days?"

Connor felt a shiver of dread course down his spine. He didn't even want to think about dealing with his daughter and boys.

"Leave him alone, Ron," Haley ordered with a shake of her head. "You have plenty of time to worry about things like that, Connor."

"But not so much time to worry about the gross anatomy exam Monday," Anne fretted, typically already worrying about school again. "Maybe we should start going over the nerve charts?"

He didn't want his family issues to interfere with his friends' study time, so Connor quickly agreed. He resolved not to think about what was going on at his home for the next couple of hours, although he wasn't sure how successful he would be with that.

The house was quiet when Connor entered at almost nine that evening. Setting his keys on the sparklingly clean kitchen counter, he walked into the living room, expecting to find Mia and Alexis there. He was only half-right. Mia sat alone on the couch, a stack of essays in her lap as she made notes on one with a red pen. The television was on, tuned to a news channel, but the volume was so low he could barely hear the commentary.

"Hi," he said, not sure if she'd heard him come in.

She looked up with a smile. "Hi. Did your study session go well?"

"Yeah. We got through a lot of material. Sorry it took so long, we let the time get away from us." He had at least re-membered to call to tell her that his study group was ordering Chinese food, so there was no need for her to keep a plate warm for him.

"That's okay. I'm glad you got a lot accomplished." She set the papers aside and stretched as if she'd been sitting in the same position for too long.

The movement made her thin green sweater strain against her breasts and rise to show a peek of flat tummy above the waistband of her jeans. Realizing the direction his gaze had gone, Connor made himself look away quickly. If they were going to live together comfortably, he needed to take such intimate glimpses in stride. There was no reason at all for his heart rate to suddenly be uneven—so why was it?

"Where's Alexis?" he asked a bit too abruptly.

Mia didn't seem to notice anything out of the ordinary in his behavior, to his relief. "She's in bed. You and I forgot to discuss it, but I think eight is a good bedtime for school nights. Is that okay with you?"

"Uh, yeah, sure. Whatever you think best." He had no real idea what time a six-year-old should be in bed, but eight sounded about right.

"She didn't argue with me. Not that she ever does. But I think she was tired. She was sound asleep fifteen minutes later when I peeked in at her."

"She didn't sleep all that well last night, I guess."

"That's certainly understandable, considering the upheaval in her life."

"Yeah." He pushed a hand through his hair. "Is there any coffee?"

"There's decaf in the carafe. I made a pot right after I put

Alexis to bed. It should still be hot. And I made a peach cobbler for dessert tonight. There's quite a bit left, if you want some."

His ears perked up at that. "Peach cobbler? Yeah, that sounds great. Thanks."

She started to rise, but he waved her back down. "I'll get it. You certainly don't have to wait on me. Want me to bring something back for you?"

Settling back into the cushions, she shook her head. "I'm okay, thanks."

He nodded and turned toward the kitchen. A few minutes later he carried his coffee cup and a generous serving of cobbler back into the living room. "Will it disturb your reading if I eat this in here?"

"Not at all. I'll enjoy the company," she assured him, looking up again from a page covered liberally with red marks. "Feel free to turn up the TV or change the channel. I can pretty much concentrate through a hurricane."

They were being so polite. Almost formal. It wasn't like them—but then, they'd never actually lived together before, Connor reminded himself. He was sure they'd settle back into their easy rhythm soon. At least, he hoped they would.

"I take it things went well with you and Alexis this evening?" he asked, settling into a chair.

"Very well. She really is an incredibly well-behaved child. She has yet to argue with anything I've said. She's almost a little too obedient."

His eyebrows rose at that. "That's a bad thing?"

Smiling wryly, Mia shook her head. "No, of course not. I just worry that she's trying too hard to please us. I want her to feel free to be herself."

"She's still getting used to this," he said with a slight shrug. Just as he and Mia were, he added silently. "I'm sure she'll loosen up with time. She'll probably throw a tantrum or something. Will that make you feel better?"

Mia laughed and picked up another essay. "Okay, you're probably right. I'm probably overthinking everything. I guess I'm still just a little nervous about all of this responsibility."

"Tell me about it," he muttered beneath his breath. "Great cobbler," he said more clearly, scooping up another spoonful. "Really good."

Without looking up from the paper, Mia replied, "I'm glad you like it."

He finished his dessert in silence, letting her finish her work without interruption. He tried to pay attention to the news reports on the television, but his gaze kept drifting back to Mia. She looked very much at home on his couch, with her gleaming brown hair tumbling around her face, her slippered feet crossed casually in front of her.

Occasionally she tapped the end of her pen against her lower lip as she frowned at a paper. Each time she did so, his attention focused on her soft, unpainted mouth. Sometimes she frowned and bit her lower lip as she made notes in a margin, and he found himself wanting to smooth away those tiny bite marks before she did any harm. She shifted her weight on the couch and he caught another glimpse of skin below the hem of her sweater. Pale, very soft-looking skin.

Realizing that he was becoming aroused, he almost bolted out of his chair, his spoon rattling loudly against the now-empty dessert bowl. "I'll, uh, put these in the dishwasher," he said when Mia looked up at him in startled question. "And then I'll study at the kitchen table for a while. Let me know if there's anything you need, okay?"

Her expression a bit quizzical, she nodded. "I'm fine, Connor. I've been making myself right at home here, so don't feel as though you have to play host all the time. I'll finish grading these papers, then check on Alexis, and then I'll probably turn in early tonight. I'm a little tired myself."

"Okay. So, uh…okay."

Feeling like an idiot, he carried his dishes into the kitchen.

If this arrangement was going to work out, he was going to have to keep his contrary male hormones in line, he warned himself sternly. He had always found Mia attractive, but he'd managed to control himself around her before because he didn't want to risk ruining a perfect friendship. Considering his dismal record with relationships, he'd begun to expect disaster. He certainly didn't want to ruin things now, after Mia had made such a great sacrifice on his behalf.

He could handle this, he promised himself. Within a few days, this would all seem quite natural. He and Alexis and Mia would all be quite comfortable together here, and he'd probably not even notice those enticing little things about Mia that he'd obsessed about tonight. Like her skin. And her lips. And her…

Damn it.

Opening a textbook at random, he dived headfirst into the pages, needing to immerse himself in science to keep his thoughts from wandering back into the living room with Mia.

To Mia's relief, there were no tears during that night. Alexis slept soundly. She blinked her eyes open when Mia roused her gently the next morning.

"Alexis? Sweetie, it's time to wake up."

Yawning, Alexis pushed herself upright. "'Morning, Mia."

"Good morning. I'll go make breakfast while you get dressed, okay? What would you like? Eggs? Pancakes? Oatmeal with strawberries?"

"Oatmeal with strawberries, please."

"Coming right up." Tugging teasingly on a strand of Alexis's sleep-tangled hair, Mia left the child to dress in the plaid jumper and white shirt they'd laid out the night before.

Already dressed for work in a black-and-brown patterned blouse with brown slacks and comfortable shoes, Mia tied on a bib apron she'd brought with her to protect her clothes while she made the oatmeal and sliced fresh strawberries. She'd started a pot of coffee, too, and the aroma wafted through the kitchen to keep her company while she prepared the meal.

Connor's books and papers were still scattered haphazardly on the table. She gathered them into a neat pile, careful not to get anything out of order. She didn't know how late he'd stayed up studying; he'd looked completely focused on his work when she'd turned in at ten.

He'd been in an odd mood last night, she mused, stirring the oatmeal. There had been something in his expression when he'd looked at her that she couldn't quite interpret. She supposed it was as he'd said—they were still getting used to this arrangement. They were all having to make adjustments.

As if he'd known she was thinking of him, he stumbled into the kitchen then, bleary-eyed and looking as if he'd had very little sleep. Still, he was clean-shaven and neatly dressed in a shirt, tie, dark slacks and the hip-length white coat worn by medical students. He dressed this way only when he would be seeing standardized patients as part of his Introduction to Clinical Medicine, or ICM, course. He'd explained to her that standardized patients were actors hired to portray real patients so the first-year students could learn basic history-taking and exams. He wouldn't see real patients until his second year of medical school, and then only under very close supervision.

Watching him head straight for the coffeemaker, she wondered in exasperation why the sight of him dressed like this went straight to her ovaries. In a tie and white coat—or for that matter in his more usual polo shirts and jeans—Connor was definitely one attractive man.

Shaking her head to clear it of such nonsense, she took a bowl out of a cabinet to fill for Alexis. "Alexis requested oatmeal with sliced strawberries for breakfast. There's plenty for all of us, if you want some. Do you like oatmeal?"

"It's food," he said with a shrug after taking a long, appreciative gulp of the hot coffee. "I'm not picky."

She'd known he wasn't too choosy about other foods, but there had never been an occasion for her to find out what he liked for breakfast. "Sit down. I'll bring you a bowl."

"I told you, Mia, you don't have to wait on me." He sounded almost cross.

"I'm serving Alexis and myself, anyway," she replied logically. "It's no extra trouble to scoop some oatmeal and berries into a bowl for you, too."

He didn't look particularly appeased.

"You could pour orange juice, if you want," she suggested. "Alexis and I will both have some."

Apparently, that did make him feel more useful. His frown lessened as he filled three juice glasses and set them on the table. Carefully suppressing her amusement, Mia set the oatmeal bowls in place. She had just added a plate of whole-wheat toast when Alexis joined them.

She was neatly dressed in the uniform with white knee socks and her black shoes, but her dark blond hair was still a mess. She carried a brush in one hand and a red ribbon in the other. "I need some help," she said to Mia.

Smiling, Mia took the brush. "Yes, I can see that."

A few moments later, Alexis took her place at the table, her hair now gleaming and tied back from her face with the ribbon. "Good morning," she said to Connor, the slight shyness she always exhibited with him evident in her voice.

"Good morning, Alexis. You look very nice today."

"Thank you." She picked up her spoon and scooped a strawberry out of her bowl.

Eating her own breakfast, Mia watched as Connor seemed to struggle for something more to say. "Are you looking forward to starting school today?"

Her mouth full, Alexis nodded.

"You aren't nervous or anything, are you? Because I'm sure you'll have a great time."

Swallowing, Alexis said, "I'm not nervous. I like school. Miss Chen was nice."

"And you already have a friend," he reminded her. "McKinley."

"McKenzie," she corrected him.

"Oh. Yeah, that was it."

Alexis turned back to Mia. "I made my bed the way you showed me. I put Pete on the heart pillow."

"That's the perfect place for him."

Her bowl just over half-emptied, the child set down her spoon. "I'm full now. Is it time to leave for school?"

Mia glanced at her watch. "Go brush your teeth and then it will be time. Don't forget to bring your backpack."

"Okay." Sliding out of her chair, Alexis turned toward the doorway.

"Put your dishes in the sink first," Mia told her quickly.

"Okay." Alexis quickly and carefully cleared her place, then dashed out of the room.

"Making her bed, clearing the table... You're certainly starting her out right," Connor commented, still toying with his own breakfast.

"I figure it's easier to instill good habits from the beginning rather than to try to break bad ones later. It's my sister-in-law's child-raising philosophy, and it's working out well for her."

"You're lucky to have her as a role model. Because I was an only, I haven't had any nieces or nephews to observe. Just the older kids I taught at school—and there were plenty of them who could have used some early training."

"I know. Another incentive for us to start out right with Alexis."

He nodded somberly, his thoughts hidden from her. He sounded as though he approved of her tactics so far, so she didn't know why he looked so broody. Maybe he had school-work on his mind that morning.

Rising, she carried her own empty dishes to the sink, rinsed them and Alexis's and set them all in the dishwasher. "We'll be leaving in a few minutes. Will you be here when we get home this afternoon, or are you meeting your study group?"

"I'll probably be in gross anatomy lab until late this evening. My dissection group is meeting there this afternoon."

She nodded. "All right. Let me know what you're doing for dinner so I'll know whether to hold a plate for you."

"Okay. Thanks."

Wondering if he was often so serious in the mornings, she left the room to collect her purse and school tote. She and Connor had decided that she would drop Alexis off at her school on her way to work, then pick her up that afternoon. It was little extra trouble for Mia because Alexis's school was on the way to the one where Mia taught.

She and Alexis had to go through the kitchen again to reach the two-car carport where she'd parked. Connor was still sitting at the table, finishing another cup of coffee as he looked over some notes before class.

Mia put a hand gently at the small of Alexis's back. "Want to give your daddy a goodbye hug?" she suggested.

Cooperative as always, if not notably enthusiastic, Alexis approached his chair. Connor leaned down to give her a quick hug and brush a kiss against her cheek. "See you later. Have a great first day of school."

"Thank you." She turned immediately to Mia. "I'm ready now."

It was still early in the father-daughter relationship, Mia reminded herself as she belted Alexis into the backseat of the car. They would grow closer with time, she was sure.

She just wished both of them would try a little harder.

"So?" Natalie leaned a hip against the corner of Mia's desk during their shared morning prep period later that day, her expression avidly curious. "How did it go?"

It was the first time they'd seen each other since Mia had moved into Connor's house. "It went very well. Alexis is an adorable little girl, amazingly well behaved."

"Yeah, we'll see how long that lasts," Natalie muttered, glancing meaningfully at the rows of empty desks in the classroom. "But that's not what I meant. How's it working out living with Connor?"

Feeling her cheeks warm a bit, Mia shook her head. "You make it sound…well, different than it is. We're just roommates, Natalie. You know what it's like to share a house; you told me you had three roommates in college."

"Well, yeah, but I wasn't playing Mommy and Daddy with any of them, either." Natalie had made no secret of her shock that Mia had volunteered to help Connor with his newfound daughter. She had said flatly that she'd thought Mia had gone too far in being a helpful friend this time.

"We aren't playing Mommy and Daddy," Mia muttered rather defensively. "Single dad and nanny, maybe."

"That sounds sort of kinky."

"You know what I mean. Did you just come in here to give me a hard time, or were you genuinely interested in hearing about Alexis?"

Her friend pretended to deliberate a moment before replying, "Both. So tell me all about it."

Mia spent the next ten minutes telling Natalie about Alexis's arrival, about how surprisingly well-adjusted and cooperative the child had been, how excited to start her new school. There had been one moment that morning when she'd seemed to be on the verge of panic when Mia had moved to leave, but fortunately McKenzie had arrived at that moment, greeting Alexis with a gamine grin and a flood of words. Alexis had looked happy again when McKenzie towed her off. Mia was the one who'd lingered a moment, watching her walk away and hoping everything would go well for her.

"She looked so little," she admitted to Natalie. "I can see why parents get so anxious letting their kids go off on their own for the first time."

"You're not her parent, you know," Natalie reminded her, bantering set aside for a moment. "You're just the babysitter, basically."

"I'm certainly aware of that."

Natalie gave a little sigh and tucked a strand of dark hair behind her ear, looking uncharacteristically concerned. "I'm just…well, this whole situation seems fraught with potential problems. I hope no one gets hurt before it's over. Not the kid—or you."

A little surprised, Mia gave her friend a reassuring smile. "No one's going to be hurt. Connor and I have discussed all the possible repercussions and I think we're prepared to deal with whatever comes up. This really was the best solution for everyone, considering how little time he had to get ready for fatherhood."

Still looking skeptical, Natalie murmured, "It certainly seems to be the best solution for Connor. As for you…" She shrugged.

"I'm fine. Really."

"Yeah, okay. So when do you get a night off? Because Donnie has another friend he wants you to meet."

Mia groaned. "I think I've had enough of Donnie's friends for now. But maybe you and I can go catch a movie or something in a few weeks. Once everything is settled down at home."

"At home, huh?" Pushing herself away from the desk, Natalie moved toward the door. "Gotta get to work. You know where to find me when you need me."

When. Not if.

Wondering when—and why—Natalie had suddenly turned into a pessimist, Mia turned her attention back to the papers spread on the desk in front of her, preparing herself for the students who would descend on her in about fifteen minutes.

She told herself not to let Natalie's doubts get to her. She had everything under control.

Why should she be worried?

Chapter Five

"Mia! Look what I drew. It's Pete. Doesn't it look just like him?"

Mia examined the crayon drawing that bore a slight resemblance to Alexis's well-loved stuffed cat. "That's very good, Alexis. I like the flower you drew beside him, too."

"It's a tree."

"Of course it is. I must not have been paying enough attention."

Alexis nodded, still admiring her drawing. "Cats like trees. They climb up in the branches and then the firemen have to come get them down. Miss Chen read us a story about that."

"I've read stories about that, too," Mia said with a smile. "Would you like me to hang this drawing on the refrigerator? I think it would really brighten up the kitchen."

Looking pleased, Alexis watched as Mia attached the drawing to the door of the fridge with a thin, square magnet on which was printed the name and phone number of an insurance agent. She would have to remember to pick up some whimsical magnets for this typical home gallery, Mia thought. She doubted that Connor would mind having his daughter's artwork displayed in his kitchen. "We'll show this to your daddy when he gets home. I'm sure he'll like it."

"He's not home much," Alexis said with a matter-of-fact shrug.

Mia could hardly dispute that. It was Friday afternoon, and after living in the same house with Connor and Alexis for several days, she had spent more than twice as much time with Alexis as she had with Connor. He always seemed to be with his study group, or in the medical school library, or the gross anatomy lab. She hadn't even helped him study; he seemed to be turning more to his friends for that since she'd moved in. Maybe he thought she was too busy with Alexis, even though she had several hours free in the evenings after Alexis went to bed.

"He's working very hard in school," she reminded the child. "It isn't easy studying to be a doctor."

Not looking particularly disturbed by his absence, Alexis asked, "Can I watch cartoons now?"

"May I watch cartoons," Mia corrected absently before adding, "You may watch for half an hour. Dinner should be ready by then."

"Okay." Snatching Pete up from the table where she'd left him, Alexis dashed out of the kitchen. Since she'd become more comfortable in her new home, she always seemed to be zipping from one place to another. Mia teased her about being part hummingbird, a comparison that always made Alexis laugh.

Mia was already very fond of Alexis and she knew the feeling was mutual. She was the one the child turned to for her every need. When they went out, Alexis habitually slipped her hand into Mia's, seemingly reassured to be at her side. She still had to be reminded to give Connor good-night hugs and to tell him things that had happened at school, whereas she frequently and spontaneously hugged Mia and chattered almost endlessly to her about everything under the sun.

If it bothered Connor that Alexis wasn't more forthcoming with him, he didn't let it show. He was kind and patient with her, occasionally teasing her a little, but there was still just the faintest reserve between them. Mia was sure time and familiarity would be the remedy for that, but she could see how it would be difficult for both of them with Connor having so little time to spare.

She had begun to wonder occasionally if maybe he could have spent a little more time with them than he'd given them so far. But maybe she just had a hard time understanding exactly how stressful his studies were, not having been there herself. She was trying to be patient, to give him plenty of space. Maybe next semester would be a little easier for him.

Alexis had been in bed for half an hour when he finally came home. She could tell by his expression that he had not had a good day.

"What's wrong?" she asked, setting aside the book she'd been reading to stand when he entered the living room.

He shrugged, his expression glum. "I didn't do so well on the gross anatomy exam today. Went totally blank on the names of the nerves branching off the femoral nerve."

"I'm sorry. That must have been upsetting for you."

He pushed a hand through his hair. "You could say that. What makes me so mad is that I can remember them now that the exam is over. Anterior femoral cutaneous branches, nerves to the Sartorius muscle, the rectus femoris muscle, the vastus lateralis muscle, the vastus intermedius muscle, the vastus medialis muscle, the pectineus muscle… Why couldn't I remember all that when it counted?"

"I don't know how you ever remember all of that. Is there anything I can do for you? Maybe I could quiz you later?"

"Thanks, but it's too late now. I can't go back and retake the exam."

She supposed she couldn't blame him for being grumpy. She

could empathize with him. She hated feeling as though she hadn't done her best on anything. She was sure she would be as driven as he was when she started her own graduate studies. "Are you hungry? I can warm some leftovers for you."

He started to shake his head, then stopped. "Yeah, I guess I am hungry. I went straight to the library after the exam and never did get around to eating dinner."

"I made a pork loin with creamed potatoes and gravy and brussels sprouts. Would you believe Alexis loves brussels sprouts? She calls them little cabbages. Said her grandmother made them quite often."

"Never heard of a kid actually liking them," he said, trailing her into the kitchen.

"I hope you like them," she said, taking covered dishes from the refrigerator. "I dressed them with parmesan cheese and slivered almonds."

"I like pretty much anything. Except coconut."

That was something she'd known already. Connor was one of the least picky eaters she'd ever known. His daughter seemed to have inherited that trait.

He studied the drawing on the fridge door while she popped a plate into the microwave for him. "Is this supposed to be her stuffed cat?"

"Very good," she said approvingly. "Yes, that's Pete."

"What's this thing beside him? A brussels sprout?"

"A tree. He's going to climb the branches and then have to be rescued by the fire department."

"Oh." Lifting an eyebrow, he murmured, "That should be interesting because the cat's twice the size of the tree."

"Maybe it's a perspective thing. Maybe the tree's really far in the distance."

"Yeah, that could explain it," he replied drily.

"I thought I'd get some more magnets in case she wants to display more of her artwork. You don't mind, do you?"

He shrugged. "Why should I?"

Because the question seemed to be rhetorical, she didn't bother responding.

He opened the fridge again. "You want a glass of tea?"

"Yes, thanks. I'll drink it while you eat. Keep you company."

Nodding, he poured two glasses of tea and carried them to the table.

While he ate, Mia kept up an easy monologue by chatting about things that had happened at school, catching him up on news about mutual acquaintances, sharing with him some of the things Alexis had told her about her day. He didn't say a lot in response, but he seemed to relax while she talked. By the time he'd finished the meal and the apple crumble she'd prepared for dessert, the frown he'd worn home had mostly disappeared.

They moved into the living room afterward to watch the evening news. Mia sank onto the couch, shifting over when Connor dropped down beside her rather than taking one of the chairs.

"I heard there's a good chance of rain tomorrow," she said, reaching for the remote. "I wonder if that's still in the forecast."

"You can stop now, you know."

"Stop what?" she asked, tuning to a local nine o'clock newscast, keeping the sound turned low.

"Stop chatting to try to cheer me up. I feel better."

She smiled at him. "I'm glad."

"I still feel like an idiot for screwing up the test, of course," he added, glum again for a moment.

"Everyone messes up sometimes. I'm sure it isn't the first time you've frozen on an exam and I doubt that it will be the last. All you can do is your best."

His smile tilted a bit crookedly. "Now you sound like my mom. Don't worry, Mia, I'm not going to throw myself out my bedroom window."

She laughed lightly. "Wouldn't hurt you that much if you did. It's a one-story house, remember?"

He chuckled. "It was just a figure of speech."

At least he'd almost laughed. She smiled at him, then glanced at the television screen. The weathercast hadn't started yet. A woman anchor with teased hair and a bit too much eye makeup was talking about a scandal involving a prominent local politician.

"This is Friday, isn't it?" he murmured, as if it had just occurred to him.

She nodded. "Yes, it is."

"No school tomorrow."

"No."

"Do you have any plans?"

"I told Alexis I would take her to the zoo if it isn't raining tomorrow afternoon. She said she loves zoos."

"That's the way you want to spend your day off? Walking around the zoo with a six-year-old?"

"I told you I would take care of her weekends," she reminded him. "There will be times when I'll need to leave her with you when I have other plans, but I'm free this weekend."

"I, uh—"

"Actually, I'll need you to watch her this coming Thursday evening. I've got a committee meeting at school. I'll be able to pick her up from school and feed her dinner, but I need to leave by six-thirty. You can make sure she's in bed by eight."

"Yeah, sure." He swallowed visibly.

She couldn't help but laugh at his expression. "You can handle it, Connor. It's not that difficult. Alexis is no trouble at all. She entertains herself well, but you'll need to remind her when it's time to get ready for bed."

"I'm sure I can handle that. I certainly don't expect you to be here every evening. In fact, if you want to take off tomorrow night and go out with your friends, I can… Oh, wait. I told the study group I'd meet with them tomorrow evening. But I can cancel—"

"You will not. I have no plans for tomorrow evening. I'll let you know when I need a night off."

"Yeah. Okay." He reached up to rub the back of his neck.

"Does your neck hurt?"

His hand fell. "Guess I tightened up during the exam. I've been tense ever since."

"Would you like me to massage it for you?"

His long hesitation surprised her a bit. She'd given him neck rubs before after long study sessions. He'd never seemed to give it a second thought, other than to thank her for the assistance.

He hadn't been acting quite like himself ever since she'd moved in. She sincerely hoped they would get back on their old, comfortable footing soon.

"Turn around," she ordered, spinning a finger to demonstrate. One of them had to get past this awkwardness and she figured she might as well be the one.

He shifted on the couch to present his back to her. Kicking off her shoes, she tucked her socked feet beneath her and sat on her knees to give her access to his neck.

"Wow. You are tense," she commented, feeling the knots in the muscles beneath her fingers. "Try to relax."

"Easier said than done," he muttered.

She shook her head and attacked the knots with a fervor that made him groan a little. "You're going to have to put this test behind you. So you didn't do as well as you would have liked. You shouldn't let it bother you this badly. Everyone has good days and bad days. Next time, you'll have a good day."

She thought he was beginning to feel a little less tense. "I know," he agreed. "I'm just mad at myself."

"I'm sure I'd be the same way." She tugged at his collar. "Unbutton your shirt so I can get to the knots at the base of your neck."

He obeyed without a noticeable pause this time. She pushed her fingers into his warm, taut skin. "Does that hurt?"

"Yeah," he grunted. "But don't stop."

She smiled and squeezed again, drawing another low moan from him.

His hair was getting a bit long, she noted, feeling it brush against her fingers. He had nice hair. Very thick and soft, the color of dark sand. Not blond, exactly, but not a true brown like her own either. She had wondered on occasion what it would feel like to bury her hands in that soft pelt. She found her imaginings drifting in that direction again now, as she pressed against the tendons in the side of his neck.

Deciding she'd better move away from the temptation of his hair, she worked on his left shoulder. He had great shoulders. Broad and strong, smooth and tanned. She knew he didn't wear a shirt when he mowed his small lawn; she had seen him perform that chore on occasion. A vivid memory popped into her mind of Connor, shirtless and just a little sweaty behind the push lawn mower, a pair of shorts riding low on his lean hips, his warm-sand hair gleaming in the light of a hot summer sun.

"Ouch." He flinched. "You're squeezing a little too tight on that knot."

"Oh. Sorry." She forced her fingers to relax, rubbing at the knot without digging into it as she had been.

What was with her tonight, anyway?

Shifting again on the cushions, he turned abruptly. "That's enough. It feels a lot better. Thanks."

She was still on her knees, and his movement had brought them even closer together. She was suddenly, intensely aware of the way his shirt hung open, revealing an intriguing slice of tanned chest and flat stomach. So near she could almost feel the warmth of his skin. So close that it would take only the slightest tip forward to have her pressed against him.

She leaned quickly backward, almost overbalancing and

falling flat on her back. She might have done so had Connor not reached out to steady her. He was grinning when he grabbed her, but his smile faded as their eyes met. He didn't immediately move his hands away from her forearms.

"Um, thanks," she said, her voice sounding a bit strained to her own ears. "It would have been embarrassing if I'd fallen off the couch."

"You could have whacked your head on the coffee table."

"So I guess you saved my life. My hero." She was trying to tease, the way they always cut up with each other, but for some reason the jest fell a bit flat.

His eyes went dark. "I'm nobody's hero, Mia."

"It was just a joke."

"Yeah. Funny."

But he wasn't smiling. She knew that because his mouth was only inches from her own. She could feel his warm breath against her cheeks, and heat built inside her in response. "Connor—"

Did he lean a little closer? Was there suddenly something different about the way he looked at her?

"Mia," he muttered. "I—"

"Mia!"

The child's cry had them tumbling apart, both of them scrambling to remain upright as they put distance between them—almost as if they'd been on the verge of doing something wrong, she thought in bewilderment.

"Mia," Alexis called out again. "Where are you? I had a bad dream."

"I'll go to her." On her feet now, she turned toward the doorway. "Good night, Connor. I'll see you tomorrow."

"Yeah. Good night, Mia."

She thought she heard him mutter a curse as she hurried out of the room.

Because of the rainy weather, the zoo trip had to be cancelled Saturday afternoon. Hating to see the disappointment in

Alexis's eyes, Mia suggested they bake cookies instead. She'd always enjoyed baking with her grandmother when she was a little girl.

Alexis's eyes lit up. "Okay. That sounds like fun. Can we make chocolate chip?"

Glad she'd thought to buy cookie supplies, Mia smiled and nodded. "We certainly can."

She opened the pantry and began to take out supplies. Even though she was dressed in a casual knit top and jeans, Alexis wanted to wear an apron, so Mia wrapped her in one of her own, then set her at the counter, promising she could stir in the chocolate chips when they got to that point.

They chatted easily while they baked. Alexis talked about school, about the friends she had made there, about the differences from this school compared to the one back in Springfield. She seemed perfectly happy. Mia didn't want to do anything to ruin that good mood, so she didn't try to ask again about the bad dream Alexis had had last night.

Alexis had been tearful and trembling when Mia hurried to her bedside. She had burrowed into Mia's arms, but she hadn't wanted to talk about the dream. She'd slipped back into sleep while Mia held her and hadn't roused again during the night, waking in her usual cheerful mood that morning.

Mia, on the other hand, hadn't slept well at all.

She'd tried to tell herself that her uncharacteristic tossing and turning was a result of worrying about Alexis, but she was well aware that she had other things on her mind. Specifically, that way-too-intimate moment of awareness with Connor.

She had finally dropped off to sleep and had slept a bit later than she usually did on weekends. She'd found a note from Connor in the kitchen, propped against the carafe of still-hot coffee. He'd explained that he was going to the library to study, then planned to spend several hours in the anatomy lab, followed by studying with his group. He would see her later that evening, he'd added, scrawling a hasty postscript asking her to tell Alexis good morning for him.

It almost made her wonder who he was trying hardest to avoid—her or his daughter. But then she reminded herself that he'd been this busy and harried even before she and Alexis had moved in, so they probably shouldn't take it personally.

They had just taken the last batch of cookies out of the oven and set them on a rack to cool when the doorbell rang.

Mia wiped her hands on a kitchen towel. "I'll go see who that is, and then we'll have some cookies and watch a Disney movie, okay?"

Alexis had already approved that schedule for the next couple of hours, so she nodded and headed for the doorway. "I'll go get Pete. I always watch movies with Pete."

Wondering who could be calling on a rainy Saturday afternoon, Mia brushed a smudge of flour off her long-sleeve red T-shirt as she moved through the living room. She looked out the small security window in the door, but she didn't recognize the sixtyish man on the doorstep. Curious but cautious, she opened the door without unlocking the glass storm door between them. "May I help you?"

The broad smile and faintly dimpled chin gave her a clue to his identity just before he introduced himself. "Hello. I'm Duncan Hayes. Connor's dad. You must be Mia."

Quickly, she unlocked the storm door. "It's nice to meet you, Mr. Hayes. Yes, I'm Mia Doyle. Please, come in."

Leaving his dripping umbrella on the porch, he entered, running a hand through his damp, thinning gray hair in a gesture that reminded her of Connor. He held a large box wrapped in sparkly pink paper under his other arm. The paper was spotted with raindrops. "Call me Duncan. I've never been one to stand on formality."

She wondered how much Connor had told his father about

their arrangement. "I'm afraid Connor isn't home. He's studying today. I don't expect him until much later this evening."

Duncan shook his head in disapproval. "That's all the boy does anymore. Study. I thought he might make a little extra time to spend with his daughter, but I guess he's leaving that to you. He told me what a special thing you did for him—moving in to help him take care of the little girl. That's above and beyond the call of friendship, if you ask me."

"There are advantages for me as well," she assured him.

"Anyway, I thought I'd come by and meet my granddaughter. And you, of course," he added with a charming smile. He sniffed the air. "Smells like you've been baking."

She already liked him. "Alexis and I made cookies. We just finished the last batch. I could put on a pot of coffee to go with them, if you'd like some."

"You won't have to twist my arm. It's been a coon's age since I've had homemade cookies." He looked around the empty living room. "Where's the girl? Alexis?"

"She's—oh, here she is." Mia motioned toward the doorway that led to the back of the house. "Come in, Alexis. This is your grandfather. Your daddy's father."

Her eyes big, Alexis gazed up at him, shyness warring with curiosity as she clutched Pete to her chest. "I never had a grandfather before."

"I never had a granddaughter before either, but I'm happy to have one now." He knelt down on one knee to study her. "You're as pretty as a picture. You look just like your grandmother, Connor's mother. Her name was Paulette. She would have loved meeting you."

"Did she die?"

Duncan nodded somberly. "Yes, she did."

"My other grandmother died, too."

"Yes, I heard. I'm sorry. How do you like living here with your dad and Mia?"

Alexis reached out to take Mia's hand. "I like it. We made cookies. We were going to go to the zoo, but it rained."

"There will be other pretty days for the zoo. In the meantime, I think we should all sample some of those cookies, don't you?"

She nodded eagerly. "I put the chocolate chips and pecans in all by myself."

"Can't wait to taste them." He held out the wrapped box. "I brought you a welcome-to-the-family present."

Mia reached down to take Pete, freeing both of Alexis's hands.

Alexis studied the shiny paper of the box she gripped in both hands. "It's heavy."

"Just set it on the floor there and open it," her grandfather suggested.

She sat cross-legged on the carpet, ripping paper with a child's enthusiasm. Revealing the box beneath, she looked up with her mouth formed into an O of surprise. "It's a video game?"

He gave a rather smug nod. "I knew your daddy doesn't have a game console. Every kid these days has one. This package came with two controllers and a couple of games. A nice kid at the electronics store helped me pick them out for you."

Mia was as surprised as Alexis by the extravagant gift. She'd rather expected the box would hold a doll or some other toy. She remembered now that Connor had once said his father was given to extravagant gestures rather than practicalities.

She wasn't sure how Connor would feel about this gift. She intended to place limits on how long Alexis could spend in front of the television screen.

"It's one of those systems that requires the kid to do active things to play the games," Duncan added for Mia's benefit. "Keeps them physically fit."

So did real exercise. And fresh air. But Mia kept those thoughts to herself, figuring he'd meant well. She had nothing against the game itself, as long as it wasn't overused. "What do you say, Alexis?"

Looking up from the graphics on the box, Alexis said, "Thank you for the video game."

"I've been thinking about what you can call me," Duncan said. "I don't really feel like a grandpa or a gramps. How about Pop?"

"Pop?" She giggled a little. "That's a funny name."

He grinned. "Yeah. I'm kind of a funny guy."

She giggled again.

Alexis was being won over quickly. Mia hoped that had as much to do with his charming personality as with the generous gift.

Duncan kept up a lively conversation as they sat around the kitchen table eating cookies. The adults drank coffee while Mia sipped a glass of milk. Duncan kept them laughing with his nonstop nonsense and it wasn't long before Alexis was holding her own against his teasing. Although she participated enough to be polite, Mia remained somewhat in the background, letting grandfather and granddaughter get to know one another.

She wished Connor was there. This was a special moment in Alexis's life, and Connor should be there to be a part of it. It seemed as though he could have taken off a few hours to spend with his daughter on her first weekend in his home. But maybe he was still too upset about his less-than-perfect performance on the test yesterday, she decided, feeling a little guilty for the critical thought.

Duncan stayed for just over an hour. Then, promising Alexis he would drop by again to play video games with her, he told them he had to go.

Mia walked him to the door. "It was very nice to meet you, Duncan."

"You, too. Connor's mentioned you several times during the last few years, and I've always wanted to get a look at you. You've been a good friend to him. Better than he deserves, I imagine."

"Oh, I doubt that. Connor's been a good friend to me, too."

"Hmm." He patted her arm. "Just don't let him take you for

granted, you hear? Connor's a great guy, but he can be a little obsessive at times. A little self-absorbed. He got that from my father, I think. Dad was just like him. My blessed mother had to pretty much whop him over the head sometimes to get his attention. You can bet she didn't let him get away with it for very long."

"Connor's working very hard to get through this semester. I think medical school is even more difficult than he expected. But he'll be a wonderful doctor."

"No doubt. Tried to tell him that when he decided to marry Gretchen rather than go to medical school when he got out of college. He regretted that decision soon enough. Wasn't like she was ever going to encourage him to do anything that would take that much time and attention away from her. You're nothing like Gretchen, I'm happy to say. You're just the gal I'd have picked for him myself."

Her face going a bit warm, Mia cleared her throat. "You, uh, know that Connor and I are just very good friends. Not anything more."

"Hmm," he said again. With a last pat to her arm, he stepped out the door. "I'll be seeing you, Mia. Take good care of my little granddaughter, you hear?"

"I will. Goodbye, Duncan."

Shutting the door behind him, she bit her lower lip. Duncan hadn't sounded at all convinced that there was nothing going on between her and Connor. She wondered how many other people secretly suspected the same thing. Not that it mattered, of course. She had never worried overmuch about gossip.

She was much more concerned about her own confusing feelings when it came to her best friend and temporary roommate.

Connor slipped into the house at almost ten that evening, trying to be quiet because he knew Alexis would already be in bed. He'd seen the lights on in the living room when he'd driven into the driveway, so he figured Mia was in there, reading or maybe watching TV.

Seeing those lights had given him a funny feeling. He was so accustomed to coming home to a dark, empty house that it felt odd knowing someone was here to greet him. Odd in a good way, he decided, but a little unnerving, too. Much too easy to get spoiled to.

Mia was reading. She looked up from her book when he walked in. He wondered if she didn't like the story she'd been reading. Was that the reason she looked so stern?

"Hi," he said. "How was your day?"

"It was nice."

Something was definitely off in her voice. There was just a touch of chill in her tone.

He searched his mind for a possible explanation. The last time they'd actually talked had been last night, when she'd given him the neck massage. That had ended rather awkwardly, but he couldn't think why she'd be annoyed with him. Unless she'd somehow read his mind and figured out exactly how he'd reacted to having her hands on his shoulders. He'd spent an uncomfortable hour or so afterward, cursing his healthy but inconvenient male reactions, but surely she couldn't know that.

Fortunately, they'd been interrupted before he'd done anything stupid enough to ruin their friendship. Or so he had hoped.

"Um—is something wrong?"

"No, of course not. I just thought you might make it home before Alexis was in bed tonight. I guess you had to put in a long day."

The faintest hint of disapproval in her voice made his defenses go up. "Yeah. Long day. I got a lot of work done."

"That's good."

He sank onto the edge of the couch. "How was your day? Is everything okay with Alexis?"

"Yes. We had a very nice day. We made cookies. Watched a video. Oh, and your father stopped by."

That made his eyebrows rise. "Dad? When?"

"This afternoon. He said he wanted to meet his granddaughter. And he brought her a gift." She motioned in the general direction of the television.

Following her gesture, he noticed only then the big box sitting on the floor by the TV stand. "A gaming system? He brought that for a six-year-old?"

He didn't know why he was at all surprised because that sounded exactly like something his father would do. His dad had accepted the news that he had a granddaughter with typical equanimity—surprised, of course, but seemingly pleased as well. He'd always said he would make a terrific grandfather; now was his chance to prove it. Starting with an extravagant gift that would no doubt be the first of many unless Connor had a little chat with him.

"I didn't know how to hook it up to the TV—or even if you wanted me to try—so I just set it there for now."

He knew how to set up the game, but he would deal with that later. "What did Alexis think about my dad?"

"They hit it off very quickly, actually. She calls him Pop."

"That's what I called his father, who died when I was still in elementary school." It was strange to think that his father answered to that name now.

"She asked about you at bedtime."

He ran a thumb along the seam of his jeans in a restless movement. "Did she?"

"Yeah. She wanted to know when she would see you again."

"It isn't as if it's been that long since I've seen her."

"When did you see her last, Connor?"

He had to stop to think about it. Had she been in bed when he'd come home the night before? She had. She'd had the nightmare, which had interrupted…

He swallowed. "I guess it was yesterday morning."

"Yes. You passed us in the kitchen as we were having breakfast, told us you had to hurry out and said over your shoulder that you hoped we both had nice days."

"I had that big test." The one he'd screwed up royally, he thought glumly.

"I know. Then you didn't get in until after she'd gone to bed and you were gone before she got up this morning. Now she's in bed again, so it's been almost two full days since you've seen her. You didn't even go in last night when she had the bad dream."

"I knew you were handling it," he muttered. "I wasn't sure she'd even want me to come in."

"She can't bond with you if she never sees you. I'm not saying you should blow off your studies, but surely you can spare a few minutes a day for her."

He wanted to argue with her, wanted to justify his recent behavior. But he swallowed the words and nodded. "You're right. I should be helping you more."

"It isn't that. Alexis and I are getting along fine. I'm just trying to help you both with this adjustment period."

"I'm sure everything will work out. It hasn't even been a whole week yet."

What might have been doubt clouded her eyes, but she didn't say anything else.

He stood and moved toward the TV. "I'll hook this thing up and show you how to work it so you can teach Alexis."

"Or you could teach her," she murmured.

On the defense again, he replied somewhat curtly, "I'll try to work that into my schedule."

"Yeah, maybe you should do that." It was as close as she had come to snapping at him since she'd moved in.

Clenching his jaw, Connor counseled himself to be patient. They'd both known there would be an adjustment period for all three of them with this new living situation. He supposed getting on each other's nerves was as much a part of that as his inconvenient physical awareness of her.

"Let's just get this hooked up," he muttered and knelt beside the game carton.

He heard Mia draw in a long breath. Maybe she, too, was giving herself a mental talk. After a long pause, she said in a more normal tone, "Okay. Show me how it works."

Avoiding her eyes, he opened the box with just a bit more force than necessary.

Chapter Six

Mia was sure Connor stayed around most of Sunday only because she'd criticized him the evening before, but whatever his reason, she was glad he did. After lunch he sat down in the living room with Alexis for an hour and showed her how to play the games her grandfather had brought her.

Having volunteered to clean up the kitchen while they played, Mia listened with approval to the laughter coming from the other room. She knew Connor needed to study, but she doubted that a couple of hours spent with his daughter would be the difference between passing and flunking.

Alexis had seemed pleased to have Connor join them for lunch. She had answered all his questions about her first few days at school and even volunteered a couple of comments. They hadn't quite gotten to the point where conversation was easy between them, but Mia thought that time would surely come soon.

As for herself and Connor, well, she only hoped they would get back to that point soon. They'd been almost painfully polite with each other that morning, both trying to get past the near-quarrel the night before.

Leaving the kitchen spotless, she moved to the living room and paused for a moment in the doorway. Connor and Alexis stood side by side in the middle of the room, facing the television set with identical looks of intense concentration on their so-similar faces. Each held a white game controller, which they were waving around in amusing gestures. She glanced at the television screen where animated characters they'd customized to resemble themselves mimicked the moves of their human counterparts.

Alexis seemed to be having fun. She giggled at something that happened on the screen. Connor was smiling, but Mia saw him check his watch once. She knew he was thinking about the studying he should be doing. But he kept playing, being very patient with Alexis as she learned how to work the controller, encouraging her when she couldn't get it right the first time and high-fiving her when she accomplished a goal.

If gaming was a way to draw them closer together, then Mia was all for it. At least for a little while. She and Connor had agreed earlier that Alexis should spend no more than an hour a day playing with the video game, and the same amount of time or less watching television. Mia planned to stock up on art and craft supplies, building sets and other interactive toys to fill the remainder of Alexis's days.

They'd been playing for just over half an hour when Connor set his controller aside. "I think that's long enough for the first session. You did very well, Alexis. You were especially good at bowling."

"I like bowling. It was fun. Thank you."

Daddy, Mia added silently. She still hadn't heard Alexis call him that.

But Alexis had already turned toward her, smiling proudly upward. "Did you see me, Mia? I almost got a strike that last time."

"I saw that. You did great."

"Maybe you can play with me sometime? I bet you'd be good, too."

"Maybe I will."

Connor looked at his watch again, more openly this time. "I had a good time, but I really should be studying now. I'm going to head for the library if you two don't need anything else right now."

"We don't need anything," Mia assured him.

Alexis left the room, heading in the direction of the bathroom, and Mia took advantage of the moment to say, "She seemed to really enjoy playing the game with you."

He nodded. "You were right that I need to try to make more time for her."

She twisted her hands in front of her. "About last night, Connor… I'm sorry if I was cross with you when you got home. I know you're doing the best you can."

Moving a little closer to her, he shook his head. "I'm the one who should be apologizing. You only want what's best for Alexis. I shouldn't have been so defensive."

"I want what's best for both of you," she assured him. "I know how difficult this week has been for you."

"I wouldn't have gotten through it if it hadn't been for you." He leaned down to brush his lips against her cheek, a friendly gesture he'd done too many times to count in the past.

So why did it feel different this time? Why was her skin suddenly tingling, her pulse leaping? And why was he lingering so close to her, his eyes darkening, his smile fading? Their gazes held for a long, breath-holding moment, and then Connor cleared his throat and took a quick step backward.

"I'll see you later," he said, his voice husky. "I'll try not to be too late."

"Stay as long as you need to. Alexis and I will be fine."

He hesitated only a heartbeat longer before he left the room to collect his books and computer.

Mia pressed a hand to her cheek for a moment, then turned for her own room. She'd get her purse and take Alexis out for a supplies run, she decided. She needed to get out of the house for a while. Maybe she was just getting a touch of cabin fever.

Connor had just parked at the library and was reaching for his backpack when his cell phone rang. He glanced at the screen, saw his father's number and flipped open the phone to answer it. "Hi, Dad."

"Hey, son. Hope I'm not catching you at a bad time."

"No. I'm about to start studying, but I can spare a few minutes."

"You ever do anything but study these days?"

"Not much."

"Getting any sleep?"

"Not much," Connor repeated with a wry smile.

"Mia tell you I stopped by yesterday?"

"She did. I spent a half hour playing video games with Alexis after lunch. That was a very generous gift."

"She's my only grandchild. I've got an obligation to spoil her now."

"Yeah, well, just don't overdo it."

"Hmm." With that noncommittal response, his dad continued, "She's a sweet little thing, isn't she? Cute as a button. Well-behaved, too. You're lucky there."

"Yeah, she's really good. Hasn't given us any trouble at all."

"She looks like your mother."

"Yeah, I guess she does."

"Got her eyes. Just like you do. Your mom would have been thrilled with her, you know."

"I know. I wish they could have met."

"So do I, son," his father murmured with a sigh. "So do I."

"I'm sorry I wasn't there when you met Alexis."

"Mia said you were off studying."

"Yes. I didn't get in until late."

"I know it's important for you to do well in your classes, but make sure you leave time for your daughter, Connor. My one regret from your boyhood is that I didn't make more time to spend with you. Seemed like I was always traveling in my job or hanging out with my buddies. I missed too much of your life. I realized that when we lost your mom so soon."

Connor was taken off guard by his father's uncharacteristic soul-searching. Duncan Hayes always said he didn't waste time on regrets or justifications. "Are you okay, Dad?"

"Don't worry, I'm not dying or anything," his father replied with a short laugh. "I guess becoming a grandfather makes a man look at things a little differently. Don't want you to make the same mistakes I made. But don't worry about it, Conn. You'll be a good father."

"I hope you're right." Connor wished he could be so sure of that himself.

"Besides, you've got Mia to help you. Speaking of lucky… how come you never told me the friend you talked about so much was such a looker?"

"I'm sure I mentioned that she's attractive."

"I knew you were fond of her, but I didn't realize how close the two of you were."

"What do you mean?"

"Well, for her to give up everything and move in to help you with your kid, even though you're hardly ever there to help her…that's a bit more than everyday friendship."

Connor cleared his throat. "I've always said she was my best friend."

"Same way I always felt about your mom."

Shifting behind the steering wheel, Connor murmured, "Uh, Dad…"

"Don't worry, I'm not going to start nagging you to set a date. But don't be stupid there either, okay, boy? Luck only stretches so far. Takes a little effort to hang on to your good fortune."

"Yes, well—"

"Anyway, I'll let you go. I know you want to get at the books. Just wanted to let you know how much I enjoyed meeting little Alexis. I plan to see her quite a bit, if that's okay with you."

"Of course it is. She's your granddaughter. I want the two of you to be close."

"Good. So when you think about it, get me a picture of her, okay? I want to show it off to my buddies when they pull out pictures of their grandkids."

"Yes, I'll do that. 'Bye, Dad."

Connor had to admit to himself that he was a little surprised by how enthusiastically his father had taken to his role as grandparent. Maybe Duncan had been a bit more lonely than he'd admitted since his wife had died. Connor had always figured his dad had filled his days with his work at the industrial parts manufacturing company where he'd been employed as a salesman for more than thirty years, and his evenings with the friends with whom he bowled, played cards, fished and watched sports. Apparently his father had missed the sense of family Connor's mother had provided.

If only this development hadn't come at such a hectic, difficult time in his own life, Connor thought, climbing out of his car. He'd like to be able to enjoy it more himself, but he was just too overwhelmed by all the stress and responsibility.

As he headed into the library, he wondered—not for the first time—if he had made a mistake trying to stay in school. Maybe he should have quit and gone back to teaching, for Alexis's sake and his own. Maybe he shouldn't have let Mia make so many sacrifices to help him hang on to a dream that he might have waited too late to pursue.

But because he was already here, he might as well study

today, he figured, throwing his backpack over his shoulder. He would think about the future later. After the next exam, perhaps.

Mia was pacing Thursday evening, stopping every few minutes to check the time on her watch. If Connor didn't show up soon, it was going to be too late for her to make her meeting at the school. She'd told him she had to leave by six-thirty and it was six-thirty-five now.

"I could go with you," Alexis suggested, watching Mia check the time again. It wasn't the first time she'd made the suggestion. She hadn't been overly enthusiastic from the start about Mia being gone that evening. "I'd be good and I wouldn't get in your way."

"I know you wouldn't, sweetie, but my meeting will probably run late. After your bedtime. And you have school in the morning." Besides which, Connor had promised to be home in plenty of time for Mia to leave, she thought with a frown.

At six-thirty-nine, the kitchen door burst open and Connor rushed in. "I'm sorry," he said before Mia could speak. "I let the time get away from me. Can you still make your meeting?"

"If I leave right now…"

"Go. We'll be fine."

She already had her purse and keys in hand. She leaned down to kiss Alexis's cheek. "Go to bed when your dad tells you to, okay? I'll see you in the morning."

Alexis clung to the hem of Mia's jacket. "Will you come in to tell me good night if I'm still awake?"

"I'll check on you," she promised. "But try to go to sleep. You don't want to be too tired for school in the morning."

"Go on, Mia. And drive carefully," Connor added.

She nodded and carefully disentangled Alexis's fingers from her jacket. "Good night," she said again, rushing out before the child's sad eyes made her change her mind.

She was only a few minutes late for the meeting. Natalie had saved a seat for her. She slipped into it, grateful that the meeting seemed to be a little late getting started. "Did I miss anything?"

"No, not yet. What kept you?"

Stashing her purse beneath her chair, Mia shrugged. "Connor was a little late getting home. I was beginning to think I'd have to bring Alexis with me."

"Hmm."

Mia frowned at the increasingly familiar note of disapproval in her friend's brief response. "He made it in time."

"Barely. You're still breathing hard from running in."

Deliberately steadying her breathing, Mia shook her head. "I made it. That's all that counts."

"Until the next time he puts his own work ahead of yours," Natalie muttered. "Don't let him take you for granted, Mia. At least chew him out for almost making you late tonight, so he'll think twice about being late next time."

Fortunately the school principal stood then to begin the meeting. Mia made a point of directing her attention that way, putting an end to her conversation with Natalie.

It was after nine when she walked back into the house that evening. Wearily setting her keys on the counter, she immediately put the kettle on the stove. She needed a hot cup of herbal tea to help her relax before bed.

Connor spoke from the kitchen doorway. "How was the meeting?"

"Long-winded. And rather pointless, as they so often are." But her absence would have been noted with displeasure, so she'd had little choice but to attend. Having spent three years working for the same administration, Connor was well aware of that.

"I'm really sorry I made you rush out like that," he said, leaning against a counter to watch her take a teacup from a cabinet. "I just—"

"—let the time get away from you. I know. The meeting started a little late, so it worked out okay."

"I'll keep a better eye on my watch next time."

"I'd appreciate that. Do you want some tea?"

"No, I'm good. Thanks."

"How did everything go here while I was gone? Any problems?"

"No. Alexis played with her dolls most of the time. She barely came out of her room. I asked if she wanted to play the video game, but she said she'd rather wait until another time. So I've spent the evening studying in the living room. She went straight to bed when I told her to, and I haven't heard a peep out of her since."

She poured boiling water over the tea bag in her cup, then set the kettle on a trivet. "I'll go look in on her while my tea steeps. I promised her I would."

"Yeah, okay. Guess I'll get back to my books."

She nodded and started to move past him. He caught her arm, detaining her for a moment. "It won't happen again," he promised, looking into her eyes.

She moistened her lips, pretty sure that it would happen again despite his best intentions. "I'll go check on Alexis," she repeated and drew away from him.

She heard him sigh as she walked out of the kitchen.

"Mia! Mia!"

Abruptly jolted from a sound sleep, Mia nearly fell out of the bed trying to scramble to her feet. She rushed to Alexis's room, blearily noting on the way that it was almost 3:00 a.m.

"Another bad dream?" she asked, gathering the tearful, shaking child into her arms.

Burrowing tightly, Alexis nodded and sniffled. "I didn't know if you were here," she said, her voice muffled.

"I've been home for hours. You were sound asleep when I looked in."

Alexis clung to Mia's pajama top, her head tucked securely beneath Mia's chin.

"Do you want to tell me about your dream, sweetie? Maybe it will help you feel better."

As she always did, Alexis shook her head. "I don't want to talk about it. Will you stay a little while?"

"Of course."

Mia looked toward the doorway when Connor stumbled in. "Everything okay in here?"

"Bad dream," Mia explained over Alexis's head.

"I'm sorry, Alexis. Is there anything I can do for you?"

Without emerging from Mia's embrace, Alexis replied unsteadily, "No, thank you. Mia's going to stay with me for a little while."

"Oh. Well…let me know if you need anything, okay?"

"Okay."

Meeting Mia's eyes for a moment in the darkened room, Connor then turned and disappeared without another word.

"She's adorable."

Mia smiled and nodded in response to her mother's comment. "She is, isn't she?"

Mia sat with her mother and sister-in-law, Carla, at the dining room table in her parents' home in Hot Springs. From where they sat, they could see Alexis playing a board game on the living room floor with Mia's niece and nephew. Nicklaus and Caroline were a little older than Alexis, but they'd been very welcoming to her on this Sunday afternoon, and all three seemed to be having a good time together.

"Is she always so quiet and well behaved?" Carla asked, also watching the children.

"Always. She's never even argued with me about brushing her teeth or picking up her toys or turning off the television."

"Wow. What are you feeding her? Maybe I should try it with my two."

Andrea Doyle pulled her attention away from the children

to look at Mia. "You're all still getting to know each other. It's been only a couple of weeks. I'm sure you'll see normal childhood rebellion in time."

"Maybe." Although Mia couldn't imagine Alexis actually throwing a tantrum or engaging in outright rebellion. Such behavior just seemed completely foreign to the child's serene nature.

"She has obviously bonded with you. She checks every few minutes to make sure you haven't wandered too far out of her sight."

Sipping her coffee, Mia nodded, having noticed that herself.

"How's she getting along with her dad? Has she connected to him, too?" Carla asked.

Mia took another swallow of the coffee to give herself a moment to frame her reply. "They get along very well."

Both women studied her expression, and she realized that her tone must have revealed a bit more than she had intended. "Connor is so busy with medical school," she added as rationale. "His schedule is absolutely grueling. He's doing the best he can with the little spare time he has."

Her mother looked worried, but she'd been wearing that same expression since Mia had told her of her plan to move in with Connor and take care of his newly discovered daughter. She'd admitted that she worried the situation wouldn't work out and that Mia would be hurt. There just seemed to be so many potential pitfalls in the hastily concocted arrangements, she'd warned. For all three of them.

As for Mia's father, well, he'd made no effort to hide his disapproval of Mia's decision. He didn't like her moving in with a single man, worried that her graduate-school plans would be derailed by Connor's quandary and openly suspected that Connor would take Mia for granted and abuse her overly generous nature. Mia had gently reminded him that she was an independent adult and that she was capable of looking out for her own best interests, but her dad was still firmly in protective-parent mode.

Yet even he had seemed taken with little Alexis today when Mia had brought the child to join them for a big Sunday lunch. Jim Doyle was a big softie when it came to children. His grand-kids had him firmly wrapped around their little fingers, and Mia suspected it wouldn't be long before Alexis had him in the same position.

Still, it was just as well that he and Mia's brother were outside repairing a step on the back deck during this conversation, she thought gratefully.

"So you're almost entirely responsible for Alexis," Carla murmured, making sure the children couldn't hear the conversation. "That must be a little unnerving for you."

"At times," Mia admitted. "It certainly helps that she's so little trouble."

Andrea and Carla shared a glance that Mia couldn't quite interpret. Were they really so certain that Alexis's cooperative behavior would be short-lived?

"How long do you expect this situation to continue?" her mother asked.

Mia shrugged. "I don't know. We've just gotten settled in. It's working out very well so far, saving me quite a bit of money on monthly expenses. I could probably start grad school next fall with this same arrangement. I don't think I'd have any trouble studying while Alexis entertains herself. I've had no problem grading papers or preparing for classes so far. And maybe the second year of medical school isn't quite as time-consuming as the first, so Connor would probably have more time to relieve me in the evenings."

"There's no year of medical school that's less time-consuming," Carla said flatly. "Have you forgotten that my older sister's an obstetrician? Her first marriage completely fell apart during her second year of medical school because she just didn't have any extra time to give to it. Besides which, her husband was a jerk."

Mia actually had forgotten that. She had met Carla's sister, who lived in New York, only two or three times, and Carla rarely talked about her. Carla and her sister weren't particularly close, though Mia didn't know whether it was simply because of personality conflict, their ten-year age difference or something more specific.

"Anyway," Carla continued, "I know you and Connor have been friends for a long time, but just make sure he doesn't start expecting too much from you now that you're doing so much for him. Men get spoiled very quickly, you know. You deserve a life of your own. What are you going to do if you meet some special guy and want to start a relationship? For that matter, *how* are you going to meet a special guy if you're stuck at his house babysitting every night?"

"Carla's right about that, Mia," her mom agreed, looking a bit apologetic. "You'll want a family of your own someday. Don't let Connor's responsibilities to his daughter prevent you from having that."

"What's Connor going to do if you move out to start your own life?" Carla continued. "And how is Alexis going to handle that if she becomes even more attached to you?"

Mia groaned and held up her hands. "Okay, you two, enough fretting. I promise you, I am looking out for my own interests here, as well as helping out a friend. Connor has promised that he'll make arrangements for Alexis whenever I have other plans. I'm not going to bury myself in his house and give up my social life, such as it has been for the past year or so. I know what I'm doing."

Or so she kept telling everyone, she thought with a hard swallow. Her mother and sister-in-law had raised some valid issues. Things Mia hadn't really had time to consider before she'd jumped impulsively into this agreement with Connor.

Most troubling of all was how any change in the situation would affect Alexis. Mia could only hope that if or when that time came, she and Connor would be able to handle it deftly enough for Alexis's best interests. Mia wanted to reassure the child that whatever their living arrangements in the future, they would always be a part of each other's lives now.

"There's one other question I have to ask," Carla murmured. "What if Connor meets someone? Another medical student, a nurse, someone in a coffee shop? After all, you keep insisting that you and he are nothing more than friends. What if he's the one who brings in a new mom for Alexis? Are you prepared for that?"

The sudden hollowness that filled her made Mia reach out quickly for her coffee cup, her smile feeling patently false as she replied brightly, "I'm prepared for anything, Carla. That's what keeps my life interesting. Are there any more of those cheesecake tarts you served for dessert, Mom? I wasn't hungry then, but I wouldn't mind having one now."

"Yes, there are plenty of those left. Would you like another, Carla?"

"No, thanks," Carla declined with a fleeting look of regret. "I already had two for dessert. But I will take another cup of coffee."

Relieved that she'd successfully managed to change the subject and determined to enjoy the rest of this visit with her family, Mia pushed her doubts and worries to the back of her mind. Or at least, she tried.

Connor dragged himself into his house on the last Tuesday in October, so tired he could almost feel his joints grind with his movements. He was overstressed, under-rested and so discouraged that he was beginning to wonder what on earth had made him enter medical school. He'd had a pretty good life before, teaching and coaching and spending free time with his friends. Back when he'd remembered what free time was. What on earth could be worth this grind?

He could usually count on someone in his study group to cheer him up, but they'd been as glum as he was today. Ron's joking had been forced and he and Haley had snapped at each other a couple of times. Haley hadn't been able to rally her own spirits, much less everyone else's. Anne had been even more stressed and intense than usual, and James...well, it was always hard to tell what James was thinking, but even he had seemed a bit more distant than he usually was.

The high-pitched, musical sound of a child's laughter made him pause in mid-step. He tilted his head, hearing the laughter come again from the living room. Alexis certainly seemed tickled by something.

Feeling his gloomy mood lighten just a little, he went to see what was so funny. He could certainly use a laugh himself.

He found Mia sitting cross-legged in the living room floor, smiling while Alexis danced around her on tiptoes, her little arms arched in the air above her. Connor cocked an eyebrow as he noted his daughter's outfit. She wore a pink leotard and tights with a fluffy pink tutu, a sparkly tiara and shimmery lavender wings studded with rhinestones. She clasped a glimmering plastic scepter in one hand and wore an ostentatious faux-jeweled necklace that jingled rather loudly with her movements.

"What's going on?" he asked, feeling a grin tug at the corners of his mouth.

Alexis paused in mid-pirouette. "It's my Halloween costume," she said, spreading her arms to give him a better look. "Mia helped me."

"You're a...ballerina?" he hazarded.

"I'm a ballerina fairy princess," she corrected him.

"Ah. I see."

"She couldn't decide between them, so we combined them," Mia explained, a smile reflected in her eyes. "We'll add some glittery makeup on Halloween because Alexis wants to sparkle all over."

"I think you make a beautiful ballerina fairy princess," he assured her.

Alexis looked pleased.

"Why don't you go get ready for bed now," Mia suggested. "You don't want to mess up your wings before Halloween."

"Okay." Alexis headed for the doorway, then paused there to look back at Connor. "Are you going trick-or-treating with us?"

He was a little startled by her question because he hadn't even given it a thought. He'd even lost track of what day it was. "Uh—when is Halloween again?"

"Friday."

"Do you want me to go with you?"

Alexis nodded timidly. "If you want to," she added.

"I'd like to," he assured her. "I'll try to make time, okay?"

"Okay." She turned and hurried out of the room, her glittering wings fluttering behind her.

Mia turned to Connor with a bright smile. "Did she look adorable or what?"

"Yeah, she was cute. Where'd you find all the stuff?"

"We stopped on the way home from school and did a little shopping. The tiara and scepter were mine. A group of my students gave them to me during homecoming week last year as a joke."

"Yes, I remember that. They named you the Teacher Queen." Despite being a challenging teacher, Mia was popular with most of her advanced placement students. She walked the fine line between being friendly and firm and her students benefited from her skills.

He missed his students. Without conceit, he could admit that he, too, had been a well-liked teacher. He hoped he would be a well-respected physician—if he survived medical school.

"I'm sure you're pleased that she asked you to join us for trick-or-treating," Mia said.

"Oh, uh, yeah. Sure."

"She seemed to really want you to accept. She's reaching out to you, Connor."

He was well aware that Alexis would prefer Mia to him if she had to make a choice, but he supposed Mia was right that this was a step forward. "I'll do my best to make it. What time were you planning to start?"

"Around six, I guess. I was just going to take her to a few houses here in your neighborhood. Everyone around us seems to be in the Halloween spirit, judging from the house decorations I've seen. Afterward, I promised Alexis we'd have hot chocolate and popcorn and watch a Disney DVD."

It sounded time-consuming, but also like a good chance to spend quality time with Alexis. And with Mia. He supposed he could always sacrifice a couple of his already-rare hours of sleep during the weekend to make up for it. "Okay. Just tell me I don't have to dress up."

She laughed. "You don't have to dress up."

"Good. There's a big Halloween party that night for anyone in my class who wants to attend, but I wasn't planning to go, anyway. Costumes and kegs are rarely a safe combination."

She laughed again. "I attended my share of college Halloween parties. They can get pretty…interesting."

"Yeah. Now that I'm a dad, I guess I'd better skip out on the 'interesting' this year."

"Oh, I don't know," she murmured. "Trick-or-treating with a ballerina fairy princess could be very interesting."

He smiled wryly. "At least it will be different."

"I'm ready for my story, Mia," Alexis said from the doorway.

Mia moved toward her. "Tell your dad good night."

Alexis crossed the room to offer Connor a hug and a cheek kiss. "Good night," she said.

Tousling her soft hair, he said, "Good night, princess."

She giggled, then turned to hurry toward her bedroom with Mia close behind.

Connor realized, somewhat to his surprise, that he was smiling when he went into the kitchen to pour a cup of coffee and settle in for a couple more hours of studying. As weary as he'd been when he'd dragged himself in, he seemed to have gotten a second wind. Might as well take advantage of it while he could.

The study group met at a coffee shop Friday afternoon, taking over a table in the back. With overpriced beverages and snacks arranged around them, they pored over the notes they'd taken through a series of six long, detailed lectures that day, trying to make sense of the overwhelming amount of new data they were expected to memorize and understand.

Connor glanced at Anne, who'd been quieter than usual that afternoon. She, too, was staring intently at her computer screen, her pretty oval face creased with a frown. "You okay, Anne?"

She looked up at him, her clear blue eyes clouded. "Oh. Sure. There's just so much of it."

"When's the last time you had a good night's sleep?"

She laughed wearily. "Probably about the same time as you. Sometime last August. Before we started medical school."

"You can afford to relax a little, you know. You're doing great."

Her frown only intensified. "I don't want to get behind. Once you get behind, it's almost impossible to catch up."

"Anyone want to move to my place for a while?" James asked, tossing his empty coffee container into a nearby trash receptacle. "We could order pizza or something."

"Sounds good," Ron agreed. "I really need some more help with these histology notes."

"I'm in," Haley said with a nod. "But let's make time for the gross anatomy notes, too."

"I need to go over all of it," Anne murmured, still looking stressed.

James nodded. "Okay, then. How about you, Connor? You're joining us, aren't you?"

"Yeah, sure...oh, wait." He looked down at his watch. "No, I can't. I've got to get home."

"Babysitting tonight?" Ron asked.

"Trick-or-treating. Alexis wants me to go with her."

Haley smiled. "That's sweet. It'll be fun trick-or-treating with her for the first time."

"Yeah, I guess."

Typically, Anne only looked more worried. "It must be so difficult for you trying to keep up with your studies and take care of your daughter."

"There are other parents in our class," he pointed out, trying not to let her angst rouse an answering panic in him. A few hours wouldn't hurt, he reminded himself again. Half the rest of the class would be at the party tonight, drinking and carousing. They certainly wouldn't be going over histology notes between beers. Maybe the study group would get a little ahead of him this evening, but he'd study on his own after Alexis was in bed. He'd catch up.

"Of course there are." Haley gave Anne a faintly chiding look. "You're doing great, Connor. You're balancing everything very well."

"Thanks to Mia," he admitted. "I couldn't have done this without her."

"You're lucky to have her. Better not let her get away," Ron advised with a grin.

Connor started to remind his friends that he and Mia weren't a couple, but it just seemed like too much effort to repeat the usual explanations just then. He started to gather his things. "I'd better go. You guys have a good session tonight and I'll see you tomorrow afternoon at the library."

Mia made a deliberate effort to stay in the background that evening, letting Connor and Alexis interact as much as possible.

She was glad Connor had made an effort to join them this evening. She'd worried that he'd be late, but he'd shown up a few minutes early, giving him time to freshen up and drink a cup of coffee while he had admired Alexis's costume and sparkly makeup.

They'd taken pictures before heading out. Photos of Alexis alone, then posed with Connor and with Mia. Alexis had insisted on taking a picture of Connor and Mia together and they'd smiled obligingly through three attempts until she was satisfied with the image on the digital camera's small screen.

If Connor was thinking about his studies, he was doing a good job of hiding it, she decided in approval. He seemed to be enjoying the outing on this clear, comfortably temperate autumn evening. Alexis skipped between them as they moved from house to house in the family-friendly, working-class neighborhood. Quite a few other families were out, costumed kids running and chattering, parents lagging behind but still on guard over their charges.

Most of the houses on the street had porch lights burning, a sign that trick-or-treaters were welcome. Alexis elicited quite a few indulgent smiles from the adults handing out candy at the doors. She really was adorable, Mia thought with a surge of pride that felt almost maternal. And so polite, always careful to say thank you for the treats she received.

Connor smiled at Mia over his daughter's head, his eyes gleaming in the glow of the street lamps. She returned the smile, enjoying the intimacy of the moment. This, she thought, would be a special memory she would treasure in years to come. She hoped Connor and Alexis felt the same way.

Her bag was bulging with candy by the time Alexis walked away from the house Mia had declared to be the last. Mia smiled wryly at the sight of it, thinking she'd have to ration all that candy over a period of several weeks.

"I got lots of treats," Alexis crowed, holding up her bag for them to admire. "You can both have some, if you want."

"That's very generous of you, princess," Connor replied. "I happen to like any kind of candy, so if there's anything in there you don't like, you don't have to worry about it going to waste."

She laughed. "You can have the sour ones. They make my mouth pucker up."

"I like sour candy. And I don't mind a good mouth pucker every once in a while," he joked, looking at Mia.

She felt her cheeks go hot as an unbidden image of Connor's nice lips puckered for a kiss popped into her mind. Hoping the darkness concealed her inconvenient blush, she looked around quickly to admire a little mermaid waddling past them in a long, sparkly dress with fins sewn to the hem.

Because she was looking away, she didn't see Alexis trip over a raised section of the sidewalk. But she heard the jarring fall.

Her candy scattered around her, Alexis lay sprawled on the concrete, her glittering fairy wings knocked lopsided, her tiara half off her head. Too winded to cry for a moment, she simply lay there while Connor and Mia both gasped and reached down for her.

"Alexis! Sweetie, are you okay?" Mia asked urgently, kneeling beside her.

Connor was on his knees on the child's other side. "Are you hurt? Can you say anything?"

Her breath returning in catches, Alexis whimpered. "I hurt my knees."

A street lamp overhead let them see the extent of the damage when they helped her sit upright. Both legs of her sparkly tights were torn and her exposed knees were scraped and oozing blood. Neither looked badly hurt, Mia noted in relief, but it had to sting like crazy. "Let me see your hands."

The child's palms were also worse for the impact with the rough concrete. Mia winced. "Ow. I'm so sorry."

Alexis looked as though she was making an effort not to cry, although tears leaked pitifully from the corners of her eyes. "I dropped my candy."

"It's okay, princess, I'm getting it," Connor assured her, scooping the treats back in the bag. "It's all individually wrapped, so it will be okay. You didn't lose more than a couple of pieces."

Alexis reached out to Mia, burrowing into her arms. "It hurt," she whispered.

"I know, sweetie. We'll take you home and put some medicine on the scrapes so they won't hurt so badly, okay? And then we'll have hot chocolate and you can rest your knees while we watch your DVD."

Nodding into Mia's shoulder, Alexis drew a sobbing breath. "O-okay."

"You're being very brave. I'm sure I would be blubbering if I'd taken a fall like that."

Sniffling again, Alexis murmured, "I'm not crying."

"It's okay to cry if you need to," Mia reminded her.

"I don't need to."

"Can you walk or do you need me to carry you back to the house?" Connor asked, hovering close by as if he didn't quite know what to do to help.

Alexis looked up at Mia. "Can you carry me?"

Mia could almost sense Connor's instinctive withdrawal. She wanted to assure him that it wasn't a rebuff, that he shouldn't take the child's words personally. That children naturally turned to their mother, or in this case, mother figure, when they were hurt—but this wasn't the time. And she wasn't sure he would believe her, anyway.

"It would be much easier for your daddy to carry you," she said gently. "I'll bring the candy and your wings, okay?"

Alexis nodded and drew somewhat reluctantly out of Mia's arms. Mia helped her out of the strapped-on wings, then took the candy bag from Connor as he bent to gather Alexis into his arms. After only a moment, she relaxed against him, her head tucked beneath his chin.

As soon as they were inside, Mia left Connor to make hot chocolate and popcorn while she tended to Alexis's scrapes and helped her into her pajamas. Although painful, the wounds weren't really bad. A thin coat of ointment and a couple of adhesive bandages printed with cartoon characters were all the treatment they needed. Mia was glad she'd thought to assemble a first aid kit because she'd figured most children suffered cuts and bruises at some point.

Leaving Alexis settled on the couch in front of the television, Mia said she would go help Connor with their refreshments and would be right back. Alexis clung to her beloved stuffed cat and snuggled into the couch cushions, seeming to enjoy the attention she was getting now that the stinging from her scrapes had lessened.

Connor was just dropping marshmallows into three mugs of cocoa when she joined him in the kitchen. "How is she?"

"She's fine. She's on the couch watching the cartoon channel until we join her for the movie."

Pulling out a bowl for the popcorn he'd popped in the microwave, he said, "Scared the crap out of me when she fell. I was afraid she'd broken something."

"I know. I was looking away and I didn't see her fall. But I heard her hit the sidewalk."

"You know what my first thought was? That if she had broken anything, I didn't know what I'd do for her. I've spent the past almost three months cramming my head with more information that I can possibly ever remember, and yet I wouldn't have a clue what to do if someone actually gets hurt in front of me."

Smiling, she rested a hand on his arm. "You're only in your first semester of med school. You have to get a solid background before you actually start treating patients. Don't start questioning yourself now, Connor. You'll be a wonderful doctor."

"Maybe," he muttered. "Not so confident about this parenting thing, though. I've got to admit, Mia, half the time I don't have a clue what I'm supposed to do with her. It seems to come so naturally to you, while I'm just floundering here."

She shook her head, her fingers tightening on his arm. "You're doing fine. Remember, I have a niece and a nephew that I've spent a lot of time with. And I've spent more time with Alexis than you have, by necessity. Going out with us tonight was a very positive step for you. I know you feel like you need to be studying, but Alexis needs to spend time with you, too, and you realized that. Considering you've only been at this for a couple of weeks, I think you're a very good father."

He covered her hand with his, drawing a somewhat unsteady breath. "Thanks. It still terrifies me when I stop to think about it too much."

"So don't think about it so much," she advised him lightly. "Just do what comes naturally."

"That sounds dangerous," he murmured.

Suddenly aware of how close they stood, how near his mouth was to hers, how intense his eyes had become as they gazed into hers, she swallowed. "I meant with Alexis."

"I know," he said, but he didn't move away.

She moistened her lips. "Um—Connor?"

"I hope you know how much I appreciate everything you do for Alexis. And for me," he said, his fingers moving almost caressingly on hers. "I don't blame her at all for being so partial to you. She's crazy about you. And I—"

She held her breath.

The sound of the doorbell from the other room broke the spell between them. She started, pulling back from him with a confused mixture of relief and frustration. "That will be trick-or-treaters," she said, her voice sounding odd to her own ears. "I'll go take care of them while you carry this stuff into the other room."

He nodded and turned to get a tray. Her heart still beating too rapidly, Mia hurried to answer the door.

Chapter Seven

As November crept along toward Thanksgiving, the Hayes/Doyle household settled into a comfortable routine. It was a busy time for Mia at school, with tests and programs and preparation for national testing. She brought work home with her nearly every night, settling onto the couch or at the kitchen table with her paperwork while Alexis entertained herself nearby. Once or twice a week she had plans outside the house for the evening, and Connor studied at home to watch Alexis. He'd been scrupulous about punctuality since the first time he'd run late, so she had no complaints about that.

Alexis was still clearly partial to Mia, but she seemed to be less reserved around Connor as the time passed. She still had nightmares occasionally. She still refused to talk about them, and only Mia could comfort her afterward, but they weren't coming as often. Still attributing them to the upheaval in the child's life, Mia hoped they'd be gone completely by Christmastime.

Alexis told them over dinner one evening that her best

friend, McKenzie, was taking dance classes, making it clear that she would love to take lessons as well. After she was in bed, Mia and Connor discussed it and decided to enroll her in dance classes. Mia offered to help pay for them, but Connor's pride kicked in. He informed her in a somewhat prickly tone that he could pay for his daughter's dance lessons. She hadn't intended to insult him, but she didn't argue, wisely deciding to let it go. He would never know if she purchased a few dance supplies for Alexis now and then, she decided privately.

So on Tuesday and Thursday afternoons, she picked up Alexis from school and drove her straight to dance classes. Mia waited in the "mom's lounge" with a book or some paperwork during the forty-minute lessons. She was getting to know the others who usually waited there during the lessons—several mothers of various ages, a couple of grandmothers, two nannies and a single dad. Even though she didn't belong to any of those groups exactly, she was accepted among them easily enough.

"I wish you would tell me your secret for teaching Alexis such perfect manners," one of the mothers said after the third week of lessons. "She is such a well-behaved little girl."

"I can't take credit for that," Mia admitted, looking up from her book with a smile. "I've only been responsible for her for a couple of months. Before that, she was raised by her grandmother."

"Well, someone certainly trained her right," one of the grandmothers said. "As much as I love my Kimberly, she can really be a trial sometimes. Got a smart mouth on her. I keep telling my daughter that she'd better put a stop to it soon, before Kimberly turns into a wild teenager, but my daughter thinks it's cute now. She'll regret that soon enough," she predicted darkly.

Connie Porterfield, McKenzie's bubbly, red-haired mother, leaned closer to Mia. "I'm so glad Alexis and McKenzie have become such good friends. McKenzie has never been very difficult, but Alexis is still a good influence on her."

"McKenzie has been a good friend to Alexis. She certainly made her feel welcome at her new school, from the very first day."

"McKenzie's birthday is next weekend and she's begging to have a couple of her friends for a sleepover. I worry that they're a little young. Do you think Alexis would be interested in spending the night at our house?"

"I don't know, but I could ask her." Mia wasn't sure how Alexis would feel about that, especially in light of the night-mares that troubled her occasionally.

"I told McKenzie that her friends might be a little nervous about sleeping away from home for the first time, but she seems convinced that Alexis and Kayla will both be fine. McKenzie's not exactly timid," she added wryly.

Mia laughed. "I've noticed."

"Well, anyway, ask Alexis how she feels about the sleepover and I'll ask Kayla's mom to do the same. We can always just have a regular party if the girls prefer."

Obviously McKenzie and Alexis had already been discuss-ing the sleepover, Mia realized when she broached the subject on the way home.

"We're going to play dress up. And board games. And McKenzie has a dog named Sookie that she said we can play with."

Mia glanced away from the road long enough to study Alexis's face in the rearview mirror. "You want to have a sleep-over with McKenzie?"

"Oh, yes. McKenzie said it would be the funnest birthday party ever."

"You don't think you'd be afraid, sleeping away from home?"

Alexis shrugged. "I've slept in lots of places. I think it would be fun."

Mia kept forgetting just how much Alexis had experienced in such a short lifetime. "We'll ask your dad. If it's okay with him, then it's fine with me. And you can always call if you want to come home early. Either one of us will be happy to come after you."

"Okay. But McKenzie said we can have chocolate doughnuts with sprinkles for breakfast."

Not the healthiest breakfast, but Mia supposed it would be okay for a special occasion. She suspected that Alexis would come home from the sleepover a bit sleep-deprived and on a sugar high, but that wasn't so bad either. She had fond memories of a few silly sleepovers of her own. "I'll let you borrow my camera, if you like, and you can take pictures."

"That would be fun."

Connor was a little skeptical about the idea of a sleepover at first. "We don't really know these people, do we?" he asked Mia. "Are you sure she'd be safe there?"

Secretly amused by his sudden overprotectiveness, Mia assured him, "I've met Connie several times at dance class now. She's very nice and I can tell she's a good mother to McKenzie. I'm sure Alexis would be fine there for one night. But if you're not comfortable with the idea…"

He shook his head. "I don't want to keep Alexis from having fun with her friends. It just seems kind of soon to be having sleepovers. But if you think it's okay—"

"I think it would be okay. But I'll make it clear that she can come home at any time if she changes her mind, even in the middle of the night."

"Absolutely. I'd go get her myself."

Alexis, however, seemed to have no qualms about the plans. The following Friday, Mia drove her to McKenzie's house where Alexis was greeted by two giggling first-graders and a yipping puppy.

"You're going to have your hands full," Mia said to Connie as the girls dashed off toward McKenzie's room to stash Alexis's little pink overnight bag.

Waving a hand to indicate the birthday decorations and

snacks she'd prepared for the party, Connie smiled bravely. "I'm ready. I've got stacks of DVDs and games and crafts and party favors ready for them. That should entertain them for a few hours, anyway."

Giving Connie a sheet of paper with several phone numbers written on it, Mia urged her not to hesitate to call at any hour if Alexis needed anything.

"She'll be fine," Connie assured her as several laughing squeals echoed from another room. "Thank you for letting her come."

Telling herself that Alexis was in good hands, Mia drove back to Connor's house. His car wasn't in the carport, so he was probably with his study group. It appeared as though she had a Friday night on her own. The house seemed very still and empty when she entered, tossing her keys onto a kitchen counter. Maybe she should have made plans with Natalie for tonight, she mused. She wondered if it was too late.

Before she could decide whether she even wanted to try, Connor arrived. "Did you already take Alexis to her sleep-over?" he asked, glancing around the quiet living room.

She nodded. "She couldn't wait to get there. I think she's going to have a great time."

"Oh. Well, that's good, I guess."

Smiling a little, Mia nodded. "Yes. That's a good thing."

He bent to pick up a small, floppy doll that had been dropped on the floor beside the couch. "It already seems a little strange not to have her here," he said, setting the doll on the coffee table.

"Yes, it does. At least you should be able to study without interruption this evening."

He pushed a hand through his hair, looking as though he'd made a sudden decision. "You know what? I could use a night off. Why don't you and I go out to eat? See a movie, maybe? Unless you have other plans?"

Pleased, she smiled. "No, I don't have other plans."

"So, how about it? Want to go out for a grown-up night?"

"I'd like that very much." It had been ages since they'd done anything together like this. And she was convinced the night out would do Connor a world of good. She worried about burnout when all he did was study.

He grinned. "Meet you in the kitchen in ten minutes?"

Laughing, she nodded. "It's a date."

A date. Standing in her room a few moments later with her hairbrush in hand, Mia was suddenly struck by her own wording. It was just a figure of speech, of course, so she shouldn't be having second thoughts about what she'd said. She and Connor had spent countless evenings hanging out with each other and with their friends from work during the past few years. Just because they lived in the same house now shouldn't mean anything else had changed between them.

Because they'd both eaten late lunches and weren't yet hungry, they decided to see an early movie, then dine afterward. They chose a comedy that had been out for a few weeks and had received good reviews. Mia put her cell phone on vibrate during the film. She noticed that Connor did the same. Was he, too, deliberately staying available for Alexis's sake?

The movie was as funny as promised, and they both laughed frequently. Mia was able to enjoy the silliness and Connor's company, being distracted by thoughts of Alexis only once every ten minutes or so. She couldn't help glancing at her watch a couple of times, wondering how things were going at McKenzie's house, hoping Alexis was having fun, that she would be able to sleep without having one of her nightmares.

"I'm sure she's fine," Connor murmured, catching her checking the time again during the last few minutes of the film.

Dropping her arm, Mia focused on the screen, a little embarrassed about being caught fretting. She must have been pretty obvious because Connor had known exactly what was going through her mind.

They chose a popular, reasonably priced Chinese chain restaurant for dinner after the movie. The restaurant, located in a shopping center not far from Connor's house, was crowded, as always on a Friday night. They had to stand in a rather long line to order, but were fortunate enough to find a table immediately in the back corner of the dining area. Sharing an order of salted edamame as an appetizer, they discussed the film, concluding that it had been fun, if not classic cinema. They'd both needed a laugh, they agreed. A couple of hours of mindless entertainment.

Their orders arrived and they concentrated for a moment on twirling soba noodles onto chopsticks. And then Mia remembered something cute Alexis had said when she'd picked her up at school that afternoon. Which led to another anecdote and then another. By the time they'd finished their meals, she realized that they'd talked about nothing but Alexis since their food had been served.

What had they talked about before she'd entered their lives? "Um, how's everyone in your study group?" she asked, unable to come up with another spur-of-the-moment topic.

He grimaced. "Everyone needs a rest," he admitted. "Christmas break can't get here soon enough."

"A little tension among the group?"

"A little. Everyone's tired and stressed. Ron and Haley seem to be especially getting on each other's nerves. I really hope they can get past that. We've all studied so well together to this point."

"Lack of sleep compounded by the pressure of constant testing has to be nerve-wracking. It's no wonder if some of them get a little cranky every once in a while."

"Cranky?" he repeated with a slight grin. "They aren't schoolkids, Mia."

She laughed. "I figure one student is pretty much like another, no matter what age. And from my experience, students get cranky."

"You're probably right. I think we're all getting cranky. We had a classwide counseling session yesterday. They made us sit through another speaker who told us to get plenty of rest, cut back on the drinking, balance our studies with family and recreation and visit the counseling center if we start feeling overwhelmed."

"Sounds like good advice."

"Yeah, sure it is. Of course, even as they're advising us to rest and spend time doing something other than studying, they're piling on more lectures and slides and assignments for us to memorize and regurgitate on endless exams. And reminding us that if we don't do well, we'll wash out or we won't get into a decent residency program. And if we don't remember all we're learning for the Step One exam next year, we're screwed, anyway."

She could see the tension building in him again as he spoke, the lines deepening around his eyes and mouth. Had those lines been there before he started medical school? She didn't remember. "You can do this, Connor," she said quietly.

He exhaled gustily and reached for his water glass. After taking a sip, he set the glass down and said, "We were told that something like ninety-nine percent of all medical students seriously consider quitting med school during the first two years. That number didn't surprise me in the least."

"I think that's to be expected. I've heard that most grad students think about dropping out at some point, too. Probably when it all just seems to get harder and harder and feels as though it will never end."

He tilted his head and gave her a faint smile. "I'm whining again, aren't I?"

Grinning, she gave a little shrug. "I understand it's a common symptom with first-year medical students."

"It occurs to me," he said as he drove toward his house a few minutes later, "that we've talked about my daughter and my med school complaints tonight. We've talked very little about you."

She laughed lightly. "That's because there's very little to say. I haven't done anything particularly exciting lately."

"Because you've been so busy taking care of Alexis. And me."

She shook her head in response to his rueful comment. "No. I haven't been turning down thrilling opportunities because of either of you. You know how it is this time of year at work—moving closer to the end of the semester, getting the juniors ready for the PSATs and the seniors for their AP tests, endless meetings and paperwork."

"I remember." He sounded almost wistful. "Still," he said as he guided the car into his carport, "I want you to feel free to have fun with your friends when you have the chance. Don't turn down any invitations because of Alexis and me. We'll manage."

"I won't," she promised. She saw no reason to add that she'd had no invitations recently that had been more appealing than an evening with Alexis and Connor.

Connor closed the kitchen door behind them, tossing his keys into the small basket he kept on the counter for that purpose. He stood for a moment in the middle of the kitchen floor, his expression hard to read, and then he gave her a crooked smile. "Funny, isn't it, how different the house feels now without Alexis in it?"

She smiled. "However did we entertain ourselves before she arrived?"

"I vaguely remember some heated games of Scrabble. Want me to get out the board?"

She lifted an eyebrow. Connor really was taking a break from studying tonight. They hadn't played Scrabble since he'd started medical school. "I'd like that, if you have time."

"I'll make time."

"I'll put on the kettle for tea."

"Sounds good," he said, moving toward the living room.

Inordinately pleased with the way the evening was progressing, Mia found herself humming beneath her breath as she filled the kettle.

* * *

"Malar?" Mia studied Connor skeptically over the Scrabble board. "Is that really a word?"

"It is. It means 'referring to the cheek.'" He smugly wrote down his score, making sure to note that the *M* sat on a double-word square.

She sighed gustily. "No fair using medical terminology."

"Hey, you're the one who added *qua* to the beginning of my *train*," he reminded her. "Quatrain—that's a literary term, isn't it? If you can use your work jargon, I can use mine."

"No fair using impeccable logic, either," she grumbled, making him laugh.

She stood, picking up her empty teacup as she rose. "Would you like another cup of herbal tea? Something to eat, maybe?"

"No, I'm good, thanks." He stood and stretched, feeling muscles that seemed to always be in knots these days loosen with the movement.

Mia returned empty-handed. She must have changed her mind about another cup of tea for herself. She studied him as he stood in mid-stretch. "You look relaxed."

He lowered his arms and flexed his neck experimentally. "Yeah. Feel pretty good, actually. I guess I did need a night off."

"That's what I've been telling you."

"You were right, as always." On an impulse, he wrapped an arm around her shoulders and gave her a friendly hug. "Thanks for helping me unwind tonight."

She returned the hug lightly. "I've enjoyed it, too."

She felt good against him. Warm and soft and very feminine. She never wore strong perfumes, but he detected just the faintest scent of roses. Shampoo? Lotion? Whatever it was, he liked it.

He didn't want to let her go.

After a moment, she looked up at him rather quizzically. "Connor?"

The lipstick she'd applied earlier had long since worn off,

yet her lips were still rosy and moist. They were slightly parted in question, giving him just a glimpse of teeth and tongue.

He swallowed.

She must have picked up on the emotions suddenly running through him. Her eyes narrowed and darkened, and she moistened her lips in a subconscious gesture that made his abdomen tighten even more. A low groan wedged in his throat.

"Connor?" she said again, her voice little more than a whisper this time.

Maybe later he would come up with a good excuse for his actions. At least an explanation. But for now…

He lowered his head and captured her mouth with his.

Chapter Eight

It wasn't their first kiss, exactly. They'd always had a warm, touchy friendship, sharing hugs and quick kisses easily and casually.

This was different.

Mia gripped Connor's shirt for support as the world started to spin around her, shifting into a new reality in which nothing would ever be quite the same for her. For them.

There was an enhanced physical awareness in this kiss. Desire. Was this a new development, or had it been there between them all along, carefully smothered beneath layers of caution and hard-earned wariness?

Even as his mouth moved on hers, she noted the firmness of his arms around her, the breadth of his chest, the warmth of his skin. She felt him shift against her and became instantly aware that he was aroused by the embrace. By her.

Somehow her hand had become tangled in his hair. She'd stroked that hair before, patted it teasingly, smoothed it into place. Why, now, did it feel so much more intimate to have her fingers buried in its soft depths?

His slight five o'clock shadow was pleasantly rough against her face when he tilted his head to adjust the angle of the kiss. Masculine and appealing. A tug of response came from deep inside her, bringing with it heat and hunger. Even as she wonderingly catalogued all those reactions, all those observations, her body moved without conscious direction, fitting itself more snugly to his, burrowing into his heat and his strength.

Her lips parted. His tongue plunged. Her heart stuttered. His arms tightened.

Their gasps sounded in unison when he tore his mouth from hers. Feeling her cheeks burning, her chest heaving, she stared up at him in shock and uncertainty, having no idea what to say next. How she should handle this development.

He looked as lost as she felt. His eyes were narrowed, navy darkened to near-black, and there was a faint flush of heat on his cheeks and throat. His hair, rumpled by her hands, fell onto his forehead. He looked…

He looked so damned sexy that it was all she could do not to drag him to the nearest horizontal surface, she realized with another jolt of startled hunger.

Something had definitely changed between them during the past ten minutes. And she wondered on a wave of nerves if they would ever be able to go back to where they'd been before. If not…then where did that leave them?

He cleared his throat. "That was…"

Amazing? A mistake? A momentary lapse of insanity? She waited for him to fill in the pause.

"Unexpected," he said with a wry quirk of his lips. "I didn't plan it."

"Neither did I." Her voice was just faintly hoarse to her ears; she wondered if he heard it, too.

"I think I've been wanting to do that for a long time."

She lifted an eyebrow in response to his rather sheepish confession. "You think?"

"I know I have. Are you mad at me?"

"I could hardly be mad when I was as much a participant as you were. But still… "

"Still." He pushed his hand through his hair, settling it back into place. "Probably not a good idea."

"Not if we want to keep things the way they have been between us," she agreed evenly.

"Platonic. Friendly. Easy."

She wasn't so sure about the easy part, but she nodded. "Something along those lines."

Pushing his fingertips into the pockets of his jeans, he studied her face, his own expression hard to read. "Did you ever think about it? Us, I mean? Maybe being more than just friends."

Moistening her lips, she glanced down at her hands, which were linked in front of her as a means of hiding their trembling. "The thought has crossed my mind on occasion."

"And…?"

"And it scares the stuffing out of me," she admitted on a rush.

"Because…?"

"Because neither of us has a very good record with relationships. Because I've never been able to maintain a casual friendship after a breakup. And because you mean far too much to me to risk losing you by giving in to curiosity or proximity or whatever other excuse we might use."

He seemed struck by her candidness. Squeezing the back of his neck, he exhaled slowly. "All very good points."

"I thought so."

"And yet…"

"And yet…" They'd still kissed. And the heat of that kiss still burned inside her, banked but ready to ignite again with the slightest touch.

"The odds are definitely stacked against us," he murmured with what might have been a touch of regret.

She nodded glumly. "You have years of medical training ahead. You barely have time to breathe, much less concentrate on an experimental relationship. I have career goals of my own. And we have to think about Alexis—she's been through enough upheaval. Our arrangement has been working pretty well so far. I don't think this is the time to change it."

"We can't go on like this indefinitely. This roommate/nanny thing, I mean."

"We never intended for it to be permanent. It's just until you're past the first two years of med school and I'm ready to start my doctoral training. Until Alexis feels settled and secure with you and we can make other arrangements for her out-of-school care."

"So we pretend this never happened."

She lifted a shoulder. "I'm not sure that's possible. We'll consider it a pleasant interlude that's better if not repeated. For many reasons. For all our sakes."

He smiled, but there was no humor in his eyes. "Very wise. Logical and sensible."

Was he mocking her? She eyed him hesitantly, unable to read this new mood. "Connor—"

Backing away, he held up his hands, palms outward. "You're right, of course. As always. Thanks for sharing the movie and dinner with me tonight, Mia. I needed the break. And now, I'd better get back to studying. I'll be in my room with my books if you need anything."

He was gone before she had a chance to respond. She heard his bedroom door close with a firm snap that was just short of a slam.

Testosterone, she reminded herself unsteadily. It wasn't easy for a guy to go from revved up to idle in a few short minutes. Wasn't easy for her either, for that matter, she thought as another deep shudder coursed through her.

But they were doing the right thing. She was sure that once he'd had time to regroup a little, Connor would agree with her. He'd probably even be grateful that she'd spared them any future regrets if they'd let things get out of hand between them tonight. As for any other type of regrets…

Shaking her head, she moved toward the kitchen, hoping a cup of herbal tea would help her relax enough to even consider sleeping.

A pleasant interlude.

Mia's prim words echoed in Connor's head long after midnight as he sat at the battered little desk in his bedroom, glowering at the barely touched stack of books and notes in front of him.

Was that really all it had been to her? The explosive kiss had damned near knocked him on his butt, leaving him hard and aching and almost incoherent, and that was how she described it? A pleasant interlude?

Either he wasn't nearly as good a kisser as he'd believed… or she had been downplaying like crazy.

Whatever the reason, she'd made it clear enough that she wasn't interested in taking full advantage of the remainder of their night of privacy.

She was probably right about the reasons why they shouldn't cross any more lines between them, he conceded grudgingly. All of her arguments were logical and credible. He was in no position to start anything with her or anyone else. He had to put consideration of his daughter before any desire of his own. And he did have a lousy track record with women—although he couldn't say he appreciated Mia pointing that out at that particular moment.

Yet he was still sulking. Was it because she'd been the one to effectively call a halt and not him? Or because he hadn't wanted to stop at all? Maybe he secretly believed it might have been worth the fallout had they taken those powerful kisses to their logical conclusion.

Growling beneath his breath, he threw himself on his bed and stared up at the ceiling, doubting he'd manage much sleep, if any, that night. Aware that Mia lay just down the hall—was she sleeping? Or lying awake thinking about him? And of what might have been between them that night?

Maybe tomorrow he would be relieved that they'd reined themselves in. But tonight, his body aching and his thoughts chaotic, gratitude was the last thing on his mind.

Mia, Connor and Alexis joined her family in Hot Springs for a big Thanksgiving dinner. Connor's dad was out of town on one of his many sales trips, so Connor would have been on his own for the holiday had Mia not invited him to her family's gathering. It had taken a little arm-twisting to convince him to accept, but he'd given in when Alexis had added her pleas.

Watching him talking and laughing with her father and brother as they followed a ball game on her dad's big-screen TV, Mia thought he was probably glad he'd let himself be persuaded. He'd certainly enjoyed the meal, putting away impressive amounts of the food she and her mother and sister-in-law had prepared, and he seemed to be having a good time now.

"Guys and their ball games." Carla shook her head in bemusement as she and Mia wiped down the kitchen counters while Mia's mom watched the kids play in the backyard on this pleasantly mild afternoon. "Your Connor certainly fits in well with those sports nuts."

Although she tried to smile, Mia felt the need to point out, "He's not my Connor."

"Figure of speech," Carla assured her airily, filling the kettle for tea.

Mia still wasn't convinced that her family didn't secretly believe there was something more between her and Connor than friendship. She'd been aware that they'd watched them all afternoon with varying degrees of subtlety. If Connor had been conscious of the scrutiny, he'd done a good job of masking it. He'd been quite charming during the meal, answering questions about his medical studies, talking sports with her dad and brother, teasing the children, looking perfectly at home.

She liked seeing him here among them. Liked it a bit too much, probably, but that was her problem, and one she would keep to herself.

Things weren't exactly back to normal between her and Connor since that lapse of judgment last week, but they'd both made every effort to pretend nothing had changed. Connor had immersed himself in his studies again, and Mia had busied herself with work and Alexis. Mia and Connor hadn't been alone together since Alexis had returned from her sleepover, bubbling with excitement and stories about all the fun she'd had with McKenzie and Kayla.

Just as well, she assured herself. She and Connor didn't need to put themselves into any more potentially precarious situations.

She just wished she could make herself stop thinking about those kisses. Dreaming about what might have been...

"Mia?" Carla sounded as if she'd spoken more than once. "Are you listening?"

She blinked and focused on her sister-in-law. "Oh, sorry. I guess I let my mind wander. What were you saying?"

"I asked how things are going at school."

"Oh. Fine. Busy."

"Have you thought about when you're going to start grad school? You're still planning to earn your doctorate, aren't you?"

"Yes, of course. Why would I have changed my mind about that?"

Carla shrugged and busied herself making the tea. "No reason."

Realizing she might have sounded a bit defensive, Mia

forced a smile. "I still fully intend to pursue that degree. But for now I'm enjoying my job and taking care of Alexis. She really is a joy to be around."

"I can tell. She's crazy about you, you know."

"The feeling is mutual."

She changed the subject. "How's the florist business lately? I suppose you're already getting busy with Christmas orders?"

Carla began to chat about the decorating jobs already lined up for her florist business. She had several customers who hired her to come into their homes and businesses and handle all the decorations, inside and out, from centerpieces to entryways to mantels and banisters and coordinated Christmas trees. It would be a busy but profitable month for her, she said in satisfaction. Which led to talk about Christmas shopping and how much fun it would be for Mia to share the holidays with Alexis, who was already eagerly anticipating Christmas activities.

One hurdle at a time, Mia counseled herself as she and Carla went outside to join her mom and the children. Christmas. The end of the school year for all three of them. Summer. New plans and arrangements for all of them. Somehow it would all work out. Maybe she'd gotten into this situation on impulse, but painstaking planning and implementation would get them successfully through the challenges that lay ahead. It was all a matter of keeping her head about her, of balancing Alexis's best interests with her own, of being very careful not to forget what she was doing and why.

She could feel the bonds of responsibility closing around her. That evening, alone in her room in Connor's house, she sat awake for several hours, worrying about the future and whether she had signed her own away when she'd moved in here. It had seemed like such a good idea at the time. But that had been before she'd met Alexis and completely lost her heart to the child. Before she and Connor had shared kisses that had rocked her to her very soul.

She had been living contentedly on her own before these changes had taken place in her life. Would she be able to go back to that existence when she was no longer needed here? And how would she know when that time had come?

"Can I get anyone something else to drink? Need more coffee, Ron?"

Connor was aware that hosting didn't come as naturally to him as it did to James, but he tried to remember to make the effort occasionally when the study group met at his place as they were on this second Thursday evening in December. They'd had to meet here tonight because Mia was out for a holiday party with friends from work and wouldn't be home until late. Connor couldn't leave Alexis alone, but the group had wanted to go over lecture notes, so he'd invited them here.

Alexis hadn't been a problem. She'd played quietly in her room until bedtime and she'd been sound asleep when he'd checked on her half an hour after tucking her in. That had been twenty minutes ago, and he hadn't heard a peep from her room.

"I'd take some more coffee," Ron agreed, pushing away from the table and stretching. "I'll bring the carafe if anyone else wants a refill."

"Your house looks nice," Haley commented, looking beyond him to the living room. The tree Mia and Alexis had decorated sat in the front window, its multicolored lights glowing cheerily. "Very festive."

The mantel was decorated with a nativity set nestled into a bed of evergreen boughs and three stockings hung from brass hangers. His was green quilted satin, Mia's white and Alexis's red. The stockings had been a gift from Mia's mother, who'd made them herself and embroidered their names across the top. It still startled Connor occasionally to see them hanging so familiarly together on his fireplace.

Beautifully wrapped gifts were already arranged beneath the

tree, although Connor had yet to find time to do any shopping of his own. He supposed most of these were for Mia's family members. She'd agreed to do his shopping for Alexis whenever she could snatch a couple of free hours; Alexis had made it quite clear that she expected Santa to visit on Christmas Eve. Whether the child still actually believed in Santa, he couldn't say, but she was still playing into the holiday traditions with an enthusiasm that was hard to resist.

His house smelled of greenery and cinnamon and peppermint, all thanks to Mia and Alexis. He couldn't help remembering last Christmas, when he hadn't even bothered to put up a tree. He wouldn't have had one this year either, if it hadn't been for the girls, he admitted to himself. Although he wished he had a little more time to enjoy their efforts, he found himself appreciating the holiday cheer when he dragged in after a long day in the classroom, the lab, the library or the ICM exam rooms. Or all of the above.

"Thanks," he said to Haley. "I can't take credit for any of it, of course."

"Tell me about it," she said wearily. "I haven't had time to buy the first gift. Heaven knows when I'm going to get to my shopping."

"I haven't put up a tree either," Anne admitted, rejoining them at the table. "I thought about it, but it just didn't seem worth the effort."

"Me either." Ron looked across the table with a grin. "Bet you've got one, don't you, James?"

James shrugged negligently. "My housekeeper put one up in the living room," he admitted. "Just a small one."

Connor was no more surprised than the others appeared to be. James always seemed to have time to observe society's formalities. Although Connor knew little about his classmate's background, he suspected that James came from money and the upper social echelons. Not that he was snooty or anything;

just the opposite, in fact. He was gracious, generous and pleasant to everyone. But there was always a part of himself held in reserve, a part Connor suspected few people were privileged to see.

It was difficult not to envy the ease with which everything seemed to come to James, who didn't seem to need to study with the same ferocity as the rest of the group. Still, Connor had to admit that James had never bragged about his placement at the top of the class and had not once looked down at the rest of them for having to work a little harder to do well.

Anne was beginning to look tense again. She opened her histology binder. "About today's lecture…"

Connor knew she was obsessing about the histology final next week, in addition to the last gross anatomy exam before the two-week winter break. When they returned in January, they would pick up a couple more classes in addition to the remainder of gross anatomy. He was already wondering how he would manage; he figured Anne was stressing about that, too.

They would survive this, he thought, turning his thoughts back to their studying. Or so he'd been told.

They'd been discussing the notes for another forty minutes or so when they heard a cry from the back of the house. "Mia! Mia!"

Connor grimaced and pushed himself away from the table. "Sounds like she had a bad dream."

He'd hoped the nightmares were over. As far as he knew, she hadn't had one since before the sleepover with her friends.

"Poor baby," Anne murmured as he headed for the doorway. "I used to have nightmares when I was little."

As wound up as Anne always was, Connor wouldn't be surprised if she still suffered from them.

"Mia," Alexis sobbed again as Connor entered her room. "I had a bad dream."

He approached her bed, swallowing nervously. He hadn't handled one of these on his own before. He hoped he didn't make a mess of this. "It's okay, princess," he said soothingly. "I'm right here."

Burrowed into her covers with Pete clutched tightly in her arms, Alexis shook her head against the pillow. He could just see her tear-streaked face in the pale blue illumination from the night-light; her lower lip protruded noticeably. "I want Mia."

"Mia isn't here right now, honey. Will I do?"

"No! I want Mia. M-Mia."

He tried not to take the rejection personally. He wasn't even sure she was fully awake. Sitting carefully on the side of the bed, he placed a hand on her arm, speaking a little more firmly. "Mia isn't here, Alexis. She'll be home soon. In the meantime, I'll sit with you, if you like, until you go back to sleep."

Her only response was a wail.

Frustration built inside him. He hadn't a clue how to handle this. Obviously, his daughter was finding no comfort in his presence. He wondered if she would respond, perhaps, to Anne. Or Haley. Maybe she just needed a woman's comforting touch.

While he was still trying to decide what to say next, she whimpered one last time and turned on her side, facing away from him, her stuffed cat snuggled to her face. Her breath caught a few more times, and he thought he heard her whisper Mia's name, but then her breathing steadied and deepened. Within a few minutes, he was pretty sure she had fallen asleep. He sat there a few minutes more, just to be sure, his ego stinging and his heart aching. And then he stood and slipped out of the room.

His friends were still deeply engrossed in the lecture notes. Haley glanced around with a smile when he rejoined them. "Is she asleep again?"

"Yeah." He snatched up his coffee cup and refilled it, hoping to ward off any more questions. He didn't really want to discuss his woeful lack of parenting skills with his fellow students.

Christmas, for Mia, passed in a blur of activities. Her school programs. End-of-semester chores. Alexis's school party and dance class party. Shopping and baking. Wrapping and delivering.

On Christmas Eve, she and Alexis attended a six o'clock candlelight service at Mia's church. Afterward, Duncan joined them at the house for a dinner Mia had prepared and to open gifts with his son and granddaughter. Alexis was already very fond of her pop, who spoiled her with lavish presents and teased her into breathless giggles.

He'd brought gifts for Connor and Mia as well. Glad that she'd thought to buy a nice muffler and luxuriously soft leather gloves for him, Mia thanked him and good-naturedly scolded him for the too-expensive perfume and designer scarf he'd given to her. Duncan waved off her protests, looking as though he were basking in being the center of attention that evening, along with Alexis, of course.

As soon as Duncan was on his way, Mia tucked a still-hyper Alexis into bed, reminding her that she had to go to sleep so Santa could come.

"My mom used to say that to me, too," Connor remarked as he and Mia tucked gifts beneath the tree a half hour later. "I had an image of Santa lurking outside my bedroom window, waiting for my eyes to close so he could sneak into the house."

Mia laughed quietly. "Stalker Santa? Creepy."

He grinned. "It worked, I guess. Christmas Eve was the one night of the year I never argued with my mom about bedtime."

"Are you sure you won't come with Alexis and me to my family's house tomorrow for Christmas dinner?" she asked, sitting back on her heels to look at him beseechingly. "It would mean so much to Alexis."

"Alexis won't even notice I'm not there," he replied lightly, fussing with a couple of gifts to avoid meeting her eyes. "I'm sure your parents have gifts for her, and she'll be busy playing with your niece and nephew. She'll have a great time. I really need the hours to read over the starting material for my neuro-sciences class."

That class wouldn't start for another week. She strongly suspected that he was using studying as an excuse to avoid accompanying her. She wasn't sure why because he'd seemed to have such a nice time with her family at Thanksgiving. Was he afraid of intruding? Was he making a point not to get too intimately tangled up in her life, because they'd agreed to keep some distance in their relationship?

He'd been pleasant enough since that discussion, and their equally hectic schedules had prevented any repeats of their near mistake, but that didn't mean Mia had forgotten how it had felt to be in his arms. Or that she had stopped reliving that interlude and secretly fantasizing about kissing him again. There had been times when their eyes had met and she'd been pretty sure she'd seen the memories in his expression as well...but he'd always turned away before she could be sure.

"I don't want to take your daughter away from you on Christmas."

He shrugged. "It'll only be for a few hours. Don't worry about it. We'll have our time together when we open gifts and have breakfast in the morning. The rest of the day should be for you and your family. It's nice of you to include Alexis. She'd be heartbroken if she weren't invited."

Mia still didn't like the thought of leaving him here alone on Christmas. For one thing, she thought he needed to spend as much time as possible with Alexis while he had the chance. Although he and his daughter still got along very well, they weren't moving forward at the rate Mia would have liked.

Was that her fault in some way? she fretted. Was she too involved in Alexis's life, unconsciously pushing Connor aside? Should she start pulling back in some way—but if so, how? She didn't want to do anything to hurt Alexis, and she couldn't be sure that Connor had the time yet to step up and fill the gap.

"Mia," he said, pushing himself to his feet. "Stop worrying. It's going to be a great Christmas for everyone. Just wait and see."

She forced a smile and nodded, wishing she could feel more reassured. Aching for something more than she wouldn't allow herself to put into words, not even for herself.

Chapter Nine

January was a cold, bleak month. Gray skies and damp chill greeted Connor as he left his house almost every morning. The days were so short that it was usually dark long before he returned home.

The cheery Christmas decorations had been packed away, but somehow Mia kept the house bright and warm to welcome him home. Candles, crackling fires, the enticing aromas of home-cooked meals. There was usually laughter in the house, and music. Alexis enjoyed listening to the contemporary pop and alternative tunes Mia favored. The child liked to dance through the house with her dolls and stuffed toys while Mia somehow concentrated on grading papers and preparing for classes.

Both Mia and Alexis always greeted Connor with smiles and reports about their days. He could almost feel the tension drain from his muscles as he sat at the dinner table with them, letting their eager words rush over him as he ate, savoring the laughter and the companionship. It felt good to have this to come home to, rather than a cold, empty house and a frozen microwave meal. Even though he suspected the girls, as he thought of them, would get along fine without him, he enjoyed sharing that time with them.

Mia had just taken Alexis off to bed during the third week of January when Connor's cell phone buzzed. He glanced at the screen and received a jolt when he saw Patricia Caple's name displayed there. His first, instinctive thought was that Alexis's aunt was going to try to reclaim her. Shaking his head in exasperation, he reminded himself that he was the child's father and legal guardian. No one could take her away from him now, he assured himself.

"Hello."

"Hello, Connor. It's Patricia Caple. Alexis's aunt."

Very faintly amused, he replied, "I haven't forgotten you, Patricia. How are you?"

"I'm fine, thank you. How is Alexis?"

"She's well. She's in school, making excellent progress there. She's made friends and she's taking dance classes."

"I'm glad to hear that. She's happy, then."

"I think so, yes."

"Good. My mother would be pleased. And so would my sister."

"I hope so." He groped for something more to say. "Would you like to speak with Alexis? She's just gone to bed, but I'm sure she's still awake. She would probably love to—"

"No. Thanks, but I just wanted to make sure she's okay. I told you I didn't really want to be a part of her life from now on and that hasn't changed. It doesn't mean that I haven't thought of her occasionally, though."

He still didn't quite understand this woman. How could she just walk away from her only niece? Especially when that niece was Alexis? "You're still welcome to visit if ever you change your mind."

"I know that. Thank you. Goodbye, Connor. Take good care of her."

"I will."

She'd hung up almost before he finished speaking.

Mia entered the room carrying a load of Alexis's clothes for the laundry. "I'm about to do a load of jeans. Do you have any to throw in?"

"They're already in the hamper," he replied absently. "Patricia Caple just called."

She stopped in her tracks and he wondered if her automatic reaction to the name was similar to his own. "What did she want?"

"She said she just wanted to check on Alexis. To make sure she's happy."

"Oh." Frowning slightly, Mia asked, "Didn't she want to talk to her? There's no reason Alexis couldn't stay up a few extra minutes for that."

"I offered. She didn't want to. It was a very quick, to-the-point call. 'How is she? Take care of her. Bye.'"

"Very strange."

"Yeah." Setting the phone aside, Connor stood to follow Mia to the laundry room. "You know what's odd?"

Opening the washer, Mia stuffed in the clothes, adding a few others from the hamper. "What?"

"When I first saw Patricia's name—well, I had sort of a moment of panic. As if she were coming to take Alexis back."

Her face turned away from him, Mia spoke lightly as she added detergent to the washer. "She can't do that, of course."

"No. It was just a knee-jerk reaction."

Closing the lid, she turned to him with a rueful expression. "I had the same one," she confessed. "I thought maybe she'd changed her mind and wanted to come for Alexis. Silly, wasn't it? For both of us."

"I guess."

"Do you want some herbal tea? I was just going to make a cup for myself."

"No—yeah, okay. Sounds good. Anything I can do to help?"

She was already filling the kettle. "No, thanks. There's more of that cake in the fridge, if you want any."

Shaking his head, he sat at the kitchen table to watch her. "I'm good."

She busied herself taking out cups and tea canisters. A glossy cover on the table caught his eye and he picked up the booklet curiously. A muscle tightened in his jaw when he realized what he was holding.

"Grad school brochures," he murmured.

She glanced over her shoulder. "Yes. I was just studying them today, making some notes about entry requirements. I'm not ready to apply yet, of course, but I thought I should start taking some steps in that direction."

He set the brochure aside a bit too quickly. He had to admit the reminder that she was still making plans to leave, to take up her own life eventually, had shaken him. Stupid, he thought crankily. Why was he surprised? Apparently, Patricia's call had rattled him more than he'd realized.

"You, uh, have a timetable in mind?" he asked, trying to speak casually.

Her own tone was equally offhanded. "I thought I'd start sending applications later this year. I could start classes next January, maybe, if they'd let me start midterm. If not, I'd wait until the following fall. That should give me plenty of time to put my finances and plans in order."

Roughly a year and a half, tops. He'd be starting his third year of medical school. From all reports, it got a little easier after that. A matter of perspective, of course.

Alexis would be a third-grader. Eight years old. Even though it seemed a long way off, he knew the time would pass all too quickly.

Mia set his steaming cup in front of him and took a seat across the table. Echoing his own thoughts, she mused, "It seems like a long time, but it will probably go by before we realize it. Funny how fast a year slips past as we get a little older, isn't it?"

"Yeah. Funny." He gripped his cup between his hands and gazed into it, having no desire yet to taste the tea. "You know, it occurs to me that we didn't talk about this part much before you moved in."

She tucked a strand of hair behind her ear as she looked at him. "What part?"

"The ending part. I mean, you moved in so quickly and then Alexis was here and we had to take care of a lot of details in a short time…" He shook his head. "We said all along that it would only be temporary, until we could make other arrangements, but I'm not sure we were prepared for the reality of it all. Of her. I didn't realize how strongly Alexis would bond with you. She adores you, Mia."

Mia took a careful sip of the tea, then set the cup on the table. Giving herself a moment, perhaps? "I adore her, too," she said softly. "And, no, I wasn't prepared for that. She was just a…a concept at the time. Not a real flesh-and-blood, utterly lovable child."

She glanced briefly up at him. "You know I'd never do anything to hurt Alexis. I want to reassure her that, one way or another, I'll always be a part of her life now. Like the aunt Patricia should be to her."

He nodded, forcing himself to say, "We're going to have to talk about your leaving, eventually. About how best to prepare her for it. Not that there's any hurry, of course. You're welcome here for as long as you want to stay. And, well, for now, she needs you here. As do I."

He saw her throat work with a hard swallow. "I'll stay as long as you need me, of course."

So why didn't that make him feel any better? Maybe because he wanted her to stay for some reason other than pity for the poor, motherless child and her fumblingly inept father?

Looking down at her teacup again, she added, "We'll work it out, somehow. We'll figure out a way to handle everything in Alexis's best interest."

And what about him? He swallowed, reminding himself that he and Mia had been friends before and would remain so in the future. Even if she wasn't living with him. Even if she weren't there to greet him every evening with a smile and conversation. Even if…

Even if she found someone else to share her meals with. To have children of her own with.

He pushed himself abruptly away from the table. "I've got some notes to write tonight. I'll be in my room if you need anything."

"What about your tea?"

He didn't want it, but he picked up the cup anyway because she'd gone to the trouble to make it for him. "Thanks. Good night, Mia."

Still sitting at the table as he moved rapidly away, she said after him, "Good night, Connor."

The kitchen looked as though a tornado had ripped through a bakery and scattered flour, sugar and decorations haphazardly across the counters. Mia winced as she stepped on a sugar heart, feeling it crunch beneath her shoe into the kitchen floor tile. Listening to a spate of giggles and chatter from the living room, she picked up a kitchen towel to begin cleaning.

"Man," Connor said, looking around in surprise when he entered from the carport. "What happened in here?"

"Three first-graders happened in here," she replied with a slightly weary-edged smile. "We made and decorated cupcakes. That kept them busy for half an hour."

Another burst of girlish laughter drew his attention toward the doorway. "Oh, I forgot. Tonight's the sleepover, isn't it?"

Alexis had begged to have McKenzie and Kayla over for this last Friday night in January, and Mia had given in after being reassured by Connor that he didn't mind. As long as Mia didn't mind if he wasn't there much to help, he'd added. He'd probably be spending quite a bit of time with his study group while the sleepover was taking place.

It was just after seven now. She'd actually expected him to be later. "Have you had dinner? I made pizza for the girls. I think there are a couple of slices left in the fridge."

"Thanks, but I ate with the group. Haley made a big pot of stew and some corn bread."

"Sounds good."

He shrugged. "I like your soup better. She was a little heavy-handed with the seasonings."

Unreasonably pleased with the off-handed compliment, she said, "The girls are playing with the video game. I told them they could stay up until nine. I figured that way they'd maybe be asleep by ten."

"Yeah, good luck with that."

A crash came from the other room, followed by a wail. "You broke it! I told you to wait and let Mia do it!"

It was the first time Mia had heard Alexis sound genuinely angry.

"I didn't mean to!" That sounded like McKenzie. "I just wanted to—"

"Mia! McKenzie broke my—"

"No, I didn't—"

"Yes, you did, McKenzie," Kayla piped in. "I saw you."

Mia and Connor were already moving to intercede.

They found Alexis red-cheeked and tearful in front of the video game console, her lower lip trembling as she confronted McKenzie, who looked guilty and a bit defiant.

"What's the problem?" Mia asked.

"McKenzie broke—"

"I was just—"

"I told her to wait, but she—"

"McKenzie never listens," Kayla proclaimed dolefully.

Connor held up a hand. "Pipe down, girls. Let me look at it."

"McKenzie wanted to put a new game disk in and she knocked it off the stand," Kayla reported while Alexis buried her head in Mia's leg with a despairing sob.

"I put it back," McKenzie said defensively. "It's not broken or anything. See?"

"But it won't work now," Alexis complained. "See? It doesn't do anything when I push the buttons on my controller."

Connor was kneeling in front of the game, doing something with the wires that connected it to the television. "Okay, try it now."

Her breath hitching, Alexis pressed a button. The game played a funny, blooping sound and cartoon characters appeared on the television screen, ready for action.

"One of the wires came out of its socket," he said, straightening with a smile. "It's fine."

"It's not broken?" Alexis asked for confirmation.

"No, it's not broken," he assured her. "So there's no reason for anyone to be mad. It was just an accident."

Alexis looked somberly at her friends. "Okay."

Still somewhat crestfallen, McKenzie glanced sideways up at Connor. "I didn't mean to."

He patted her red head. "I know you didn't. Don't worry about it. What were you girls playing?"

"We were playing the Barbie game, but we wanted to do the bowling game," Kayla replied.

"I told McKenzie that Mia would change the disk for us, but she had to try to do it herself," Alexis murmured.

Mia touched Alexis's shoulder. "Be a gracious hostess," she

murmured, just for Alexis's ears. "Don't make McKenzie feel worse, okay?"

Alexis bit her lip, looking on the verge of tears again and making Mia realize just how rare it was that she had to correct the child's behavior.

"I'll put the bowling game in for you," Connor offered quickly.

"I don't know how to play," Kayla said.

"I'll show you. Want me to play a couple of games with you?"

McKenzie's face brightened. "That would be fun."

Alexis looked up at Mia. "Will you play, too?"

"I need to clean the kitchen. Play with your friends and your daddy, and then we'll all have a cupcake, okay?"

Nodding, Alexis rejoined the others. Giving Connor an encouraging smile over the three little heads, Mia turned back to the kitchen.

An hour later, Connor was closed in his room and the girls sat around the kitchen table, eating the cupcakes they had decorated. Mia had provided pink frosting and assorted candies and sprinkles, and the girls had applied them liberally. Wreathed in smiles again, their little faces were amusingly smeared with the results of their culinary artwork.

Connor had snagged one of the cakes, along with a cup of coffee, to munch while he studied. Mia hadn't been able to resist smiling when he'd studied the assortment of cakes with their thickly applied frosting, mounds of sprinkles and crookedly stuck-on candy hearts. He'd carefully selected one that Alexis had decorated, though he assured her friends that theirs were just as appealing.

"Your dad's pretty cool," McKenzie told Alexis around a mouthful of cake. "He's good at video games, isn't he?"

Alexis nodded. "He knows everything about it."

"My daddy's awful at video games," Kayla grumbled with a roll of her eyes. "My big brother Patrick says our daddy is technally challenged."

Technally? Mia had to think about that for just a moment before translating it to technologically challenged.

"I'm technally challenged, myself," she said with a slight laugh. "Alexis and her dad beat me every time I play with them."

"Daddy always wins," Alexis said, preening a little for her friends. "He's probably the best video game player ever."

"Patrick could beat him," Kayla mused. "My mom says Patrick's obsessed with video games. She always says she's going to throw the games in the street, but she never does."

Stifling a smile, Mia took a sip of her tea.

"My daddy could beat him, I bet," Alexis argued. "He's going to be a doctor."

Mia quickly changed the subject before it turned into a who's-better debate, but she was a little surprised by Alexis's behavior that evening. She was acting…well, like a six-year-old. Fussing with her friends and bragging about her father; typical behavior for other children, but rather new coming from Alexis.

Although she made a mental note not to let her push the boundaries too much, Mia was just a tiny bit relieved to see Alexis acting more like a regular child than someone who'd experienced far too much in her few, short years.

She was also pleased that Alexis spoke so proudly of Connor to her friends. Mia would have to tell him later that his daughter considered him one of the all-time great video gamers. He'd probably get a kick out of that.

Remembering the way he'd looked in the living room, laughing and surrounded by admiring little girls, she resisted a sudden, exasperating urge to fan her overly warm cheeks.

An ice storm during the first Sunday of February brought life to a full stop in the Little Rock area. The roads were slick and hazardous and local police begged motorists to stay off the streets.

Having stocked up on groceries because of the weather forecasts, Mia made a big pot of vegetable soup and some healthy oatmeal-raisin cookies. Connor was glad he had a gas stove. If the power went out, as he worried it might, they wouldn't go hungry and they could heat water, if necessary.

Housebound because of the road conditions and because he didn't want to risk leaving Mia and Alexis alone in case of problems, he spread his papers on the kitchen table and bent over them for the afternoon. At least he could catch up on lecture notes during this unexpected day at home. Mia set Alexis down with colored paper, crayons, scissors, glue and stickers, spreading an old sheet so the child could make as big a mess as she liked with her crafting. And then Mia sat on the couch with a book she'd been wanting to read.

It was a quiet afternoon, broken only by the sound of ice hitting the windows, the occasional crack of a breaking tree branch outside, Alexis humming to herself as she played. Connor's phone rang a few times as Anne and then Ron called in with study questions, but he handled those calls quickly and went back to work.

Realizing he hadn't heard sounds from Alexis in a while, he looked up later that afternoon to see that she'd fallen asleep curled on the rug in front of the fire. Her crafts and toys were spread around her, and Mia had covered her with a brightly striped throw.

"She's out, huh?" he asked quietly, stretching kinks out of his muscles.

Her voice as soft as his, Mia replied, "She nodded off about twenty minutes ago. You were so wrapped up in your notes I figured you didn't notice."

"I didn't," he admitted. "Is there any more coffee?"

She set her book aside and stood. "No, but I'll make some."

He was already on his feet. "You don't have to get up. I can make it."

"I need to move around a little, anyway. I'm not used to sitting in one place that long."

He opened a cabinet to take out the coffee while Mia rinsed the pot. "How's your book?"

"It's good. Very suspenseful."

"Glad you're enjoying it."

"Yes. I don't find enough time to read just for pleasure."

They had started the coffeemaker when the lights flickered. Mia glanced around nervously. "I hope the power doesn't go out."

"We've got supplies if it does. Hope it waits until this coffee is brewed, though," he added with a wry smile. He warmed the insulated carafe with hot water so it would hold the heat of the coffee better when he filled it. If the power went out, he'd at least have a carafe of coffee that would stay warm for a few hours.

The lights flickered again and they both held their breath for a moment. When nothing more happened, they exchanged smiles of relief. Connor plucked a banana from a bunch hanging from a stainless steel holder on the counter and began to peel it.

"At least the temperature is supposed to rise above freezing tomorrow afternoon," he commented. "The ice shouldn't last long. Doubt that schools will be open tomorrow, though, because the morning commute's going to be bad."

"As long as the power stays on…"

"Maybe it will." Finishing the banana in three big bites, he tossed the peel into the garbage. "Want some coffee?"

"Yes, thank you."

He filled cups for both of them, then poured the rest into the carafe. He had just turned to hand Mia her coffee when the lights flickered again, and then the room was pitched into darkness.

It was just after 5 p.m., but between the short winter day and the heavily clouded skies, it might as well have been midnight. Not a glimmer of light came through the curtained windows. A faint glow from the direction of the living room came from the fire, but that light didn't penetrate into where they stood.

He heard Mia inhale on a hiss. "What's wrong?"

"I spilled coffee on my hand. Stupid."

Fumbling to set his own cup on the counter, he reached carefully for hers. "Give me your cup. How bad is the burn?"

"Not too bad. Just stings."

He was sure it did. The coffee was still very hot.

Together, they managed to set down her cup. Groping in the darkness, Connor turned on the cold water at the sink and instructed Mia to give him her scalded hand. With his arm around her shoulders, he guided her hand into the flow to make sure all the hot coffee was washed off.

"Does that feel better?" he asked, wishing he could see the extent of the damage. He'd set out a couple of electric lanterns in case they needed them, but of course they were out of reach, he thought with an exasperated shake of his head. One sat in the living room, the other on the table near his books.

"I'm fine, Connor," she assured him. "It was just a few drops. Probably no more than a couple of red dots on my skin. I hardly even feel them now."

He turned off the water and groped for a paper towel so they could dry off. He dabbed at her hand, himself, his head close to hers in the shadows. "Just stand here while I make my way to the electric lantern," he instructed. "No need for us both to go stumbling around in the dark."

She laughed quietly, her breath brushing his cheek. "There's never a flashlight within reach in these situations, is there?"

"There's a flashlight in the drawer by the stove. I meant to set it out on the counter, but I forgot. I can probably get to the lantern before I can find the flashlight."

"Okay. I'll wait until you get it and then we'll pull out the flashlight and light some candles and…um."

Maybe she'd just become aware of how closely they stood. His head bent over hers, his hands still holding hers, their breath intermingling. Without the hum of electrical appliances, it was so quiet in the room that he could almost hear his own heart beating, the rate quickening.

"Connor—"

It was easier than he might have expected to find her mouth in the darkness. His lips closed over hers with accuracy and after a fraction of a second of hesitation, hers parted in welcome. She made a little sound at the back of her throat. Before he could decide if it was protest or pleasure, she wrapped her arms around his neck and pulled him more deeply into the kiss.

He slid his hands down her slender back, stopping at the curve of her hips to settle her against him. There was no hiding his response to her; he didn't even try. It seemed the more he tried to fight his reactions to her, the stronger they became.

If she didn't know by now that his feelings for her had been undergoing a change during the past few months, then she simply hadn't been paying close enough attention.

He plunged his tongue into her mouth, savoring the taste of her. She murmured again and tightened her fingers around his neck, her fingertips buried in his hair. Unbidden, his mind filled with thoughts of those soft hands on his bare back, gripping his shoulders, sliding down to his hips. The images swirled in his head until he'd lost any semblance of coherency. Lights flashed behind his eyelids, but they weren't generated by the power company, rather by the heat building between him and Mia.

She drew in a shuddering breath when he released her mouth, his forehead resting against hers. "We weren't going to do that again."

His own voice was gravelly. "I didn't plan on it."

"I know." She unlocked her clasp around his neck, but didn't move away from him. Instead, her hands slid down to grip the front of his shirt as he continued to hold her. "I don't know how to handle this."

Her rather plaintive confession made his chest ache. She

sounded confused, a little afraid. Even though that was hardly the reaction he wanted from her, he certainly understood, because he felt much the same way himself.

"Maybe we should just keep taking it a day at a time," he suggested after clearing his throat. "You know, just…see what happens."

"That sounds a little risky."

He forced himself to drop his arms, taking a step backward. Making hard contact with the counter behind him, he swallowed a curse.

Steadying himself quickly, he said, "There's no need to try to analyze or categorize what happened, is there? I mean, it was a kiss. It's understandable, considering the circumstances."

"Considering the circumstances?" she repeated, as if she wasn't sure she'd heard him correctly. Whatever heat had been in her voice before was cooling as rapidly as the room around them.

He was making a real mess of this. Again. "Mia, I—"

Pushing a hand through his hair, he thought about getting the lantern before he continued. But maybe this would be easier in the dark. "I just don't want you to think I'm trying to push you into anything. We live together and we have a normal, healthy attraction to each other. We can deal with that, right? There's no need for anything to change significantly, for either of us."

He was trying to reassure her. Trying to let her know there was no need to be concerned that he wanted to tie her down. In his experience, women didn't like to feel tied down.

So why was he feeling waves of irritation coming from her direction? He still couldn't see her expression, but he had the distinct impression that she was scowling.

He really was bad at this sort of thing, he thought in self-disgust. "Mia—"

"Mia? Where are you? Why aren't the lights on?"

"I'm in here, Alexis," she called out, her voice steady and

reassuring now. "The power's out. Stay where you are and your dad and I will find some flashlights and candles, okay?"

"Okay."

"Why don't you get that lantern you were talking about," Mia suggested to Connor. "I'm getting really tired of stumbling around in the dark."

Wincing, he wished he spoke female a little more fluently. There was obviously a message conveyed in that sentiment— but damned if he knew what it was.

A few short hours later, Connor stood in the doorway of the living room, having just returned from a flashlight-guided trek to his bedroom to fetch another blanket.

He was struck motionless by the sight that lay in front of him. He'd pulled out an old air mattress he had used as a bed in the apartment he'd lived in briefly after his divorce. He'd inflated it and set it in front of the fireplace for Mia and Alexis to share. He planned to take the couch for the night, at least until the power came back on to heat the rest of the house again.

Mia and Alexis snuggled together on the air mattress, their heads close together on their pillows, blankets pulled to their chins against the chill in the room that the small fire couldn't entirely dispel. To save the batteries in the electric lanterns, they'd turned them off, leaving the room illuminated by the fire and by a few emergency candles in heavy, safe jars. As the soft light flickered across their faces, Mia and Alexis talked in quiet voices, both laughing at something silly they were saying.

He had the sensation of something sharp stabbing him right through the chest. Directly into the vicinity of his heart.

He loved her, he thought in a daze. He didn't even bother to clarify which one he meant. He loved them both.

His fingers tightened spasmodically on the blanket as a ripple of fear followed the bolt of realization.

He had never been lucky in love. The women he'd loved in

the past had all left him. His mother, through no choice of her own, of course. Brandy and Gretchen, fully of their own volition.

Now there was Mia, who had come to him in generosity and sympathy, putting her own plans on hold, but not forgotten. How long could he really expect her to stay? It wasn't as if he had much to offer her in return for the foreseeable future.

"Why are you just standing there, Daddy?" Alexis asked, drowsily teasing. "Aren't you going to sleep on the couch?"

Daddy. It still sounded funny to him when she called him that. She was getting more comfortable with him, though he had no doubt that her heart belonged primarily to Mia. Certainly understandable—but how would she cope when Mia moved on? How would he make up for that loss, when he could hardly bear to think about that time, himself? Why hadn't he anticipated this complication when he'd blithely accepted Mia's offer of help?

Pushing the anxiety to the back of his mind, he moved forward, trying to speak normally. "Yeah. I was taking a look around. Checking stuff," he added vaguely, tossing the blanket on the couch.

"You know, I'm not really sleepy right now," he said, aiming the flashlight toward the kitchen. "I think I'll study by lantern light for a little longer, if it won't bother either of you."

"You won't bother us," Mia assured him, her expression shuttered in the flickering shadows. "Alexis and I are going to tell each other stories until we fall asleep. But we'll keep it down, so we don't disturb your studying."

"No need for that." He moved carefully across the room toward the kitchen.

"I like hearing you talking in here," he added with a candidness that rather surprised even him. "It makes me feel less alone."

Alexis laughed softly. "Are you afraid of the dark, Daddy?"

His mouth twisted. "Yeah, princess. I guess I am."

"Don't worry," she told him, her sweet little smile twisting his heart again. "We'll be right here."

He nodded, taking one last look at them there before turning back to his books and papers.

They were all here. For now. But for how much longer?

Normal, healthy attraction.
No need for anything to change.

Snippets of things Connor had said in the kitchen kept running through Mia's head as she lay on the air mattress, staring at the fire and wishing she could escape into sleep. Alexis slept soundly beside her, and Mia could still hear Connor moving around in the kitchen, but she had no desire to slip out of the covers to join him.

No need to risk any further humiliation for one evening.

What had she expected? she asked herself, scowling into the flames. That a few kisses would solve all the issues between her and Connor?

He had told her all along that he wasn't in a position to offer anything more than friendship. It had been difficult enough for him to take Alexis into his life on a permanent basis, even though he'd felt he had no other choice about that. He certainly wasn't making any more commitments that would interfere with his all-consuming plans.

She reminded herself that she had entered this situation willingly. That the idea had been hers and hers alone. Sure, she'd been naive. Unprepared for the reality of caring for a child. Of loving that child and being loved in return. Of living with the man she had considered her best friend. She'd foolishly believed the attraction she had always felt for him would be something she could keep to herself, a silly little secret that would have no effect on their relationship.

What she hadn't expected was that she would feel an answering attraction.

Proximity. That was his explanation for the kisses they had shared. A healthy man sharing living quarters with a woman he found attractive—it was only logical, in his infuriatingly male logic, that they would occasionally act on that attraction. And having done so, they should be able to continue as they'd been before, with no important changes to their friendship, as he'd suggested.

Stupid man.

Alexis stirred in her sleep, murmuring something beneath her breath. Mia smoothed the child's hair, her heart twisting with love and pain. She really hadn't known what she was getting into when she'd moved in here, she thought again, staring blindly at the leaping flames in front of her. Had she had even a clue of the heartache she would face, would she make that same choice again?

Chapter Ten

"You have to meet this guy, Mia. He's so cute. Wait till you see his eyes. They're so dark a girl could get lost in them. And his eyelashes—well, let's just say I'm very jealous of his eyelashes."

"He sounds very attractive."

Natalie made a rude sound and pointed at Mia with half a peanut butter sandwich. They sat at a small, round table in the otherwise empty teachers' lounge, both being blessedly free from lunchroom duty that day. Although a welcome retreat from students, the lounge was hardly luxurious. It was furnished with a couple of worn couches, this little table and four chairs, a soda machine, a fridge, and a long counter that held a sink, a small microwave and a coffeepot that someone always drained without refilling.

"Have you not been listening to me? He's not just attractive. He's gorgeous. I'm telling you, if I weren't seeing Donnie, I'd jump this guy in a New York minute. His name is Cliff, by the way. Cliff Duffie. Isn't that the cutest name?"

"Adorable. But, seriously, Nat, I'm just not in the mood to meet anyone new right now. There's just too much going on here at school and at home and…well, you know. Bad time."

Natalie made a sound that was suspiciously like a growl. "That's what you always say these days. Do you know how long it's been since we've been out after school?"

Feeling a bit guilty, Mia shifted in her seat. "It's not that I don't want to hang out with you. I just don't really want to go on a blind date. Why don't you and I plan to do something, just the two of us? Dinner or a movie or something? Or we could drive out to that new shopping center. You've been wanting to see what's there, haven't you?"

Eyeing her speculatively, Natalie took another bite of her sandwich, chewed and swallowed before speaking again. "What's going on, Mia? You've been acting differently for a couple of weeks. Ever since that ice storm, really. Are you and Connor having problems? I warned you it would be difficult with all of you living in that little house. Starting to wear on each other's nerves?"

Glancing around to make sure no one was eavesdropping on their conversation in the tiny lounge, Mia shook her head. "No, it isn't like that. I've hardly even seen Connor for the past weeks. He's always with his study group or in the lab or the library. Ever since he started these two new classes, he's busier than ever."

"So that's the problem? You're feeling neglected? Taken for granted, maybe?"

"There's no problem," Mia insisted with a shake of her head, pushing away her own barely touched lunch. "It's just…I guess a touch of winter blues. I'm ready for spring."

"What about summer break? You'll have more time for yourself then, won't you? Medical school isn't in session in summer, right?"

"Connor has a couple of months off school. He told me he's

doing something called a preceptorship. Basically, shadowing in a family practice clinic."

"That's what he wants to do? Family practice?"

"Last I heard." Not that she'd talked to him much lately, she thought glumly. "There's a huge demand for family practice doctors as opposed to specialists. They don't make as much money, but that isn't why Connor is going into this, as we've already discussed."

"I still think he should have stuck with teaching," Natalie murmured. "That's another field with huge demand. And because money supposedly doesn't matter to him, he shouldn't mind living on a teacher's salary."

"He wants to be a doctor."

"Hmm. Wants it badly enough to sacrifice a lot for it, apparently."

Mia frowned. "What do you mean?"

"Come on, Mia. Look at the hours he's already put into this. His old friends here at the school never see him anymore. Coach Johnson told me the other day that he felt as though Connor had dropped off the face of the earth, and they were pretty tight when Connor worked here. And I know his other old buddies feel the same way."

"He just doesn't have time."

"He's got a kid he hardly sees, leaving you completely responsible for her. You're trying to do your work, prepare for your future and take care of his daughter all at the same time, and the strain is showing on you. You never go out, you don't seem as happy as you used to be, you're blowing off chances to meet guys who could have something to offer you other than an unpaid housekeeping position, you know?"

"Oh, come on, Natalie, that isn't—"

Some sixth sense made Mia aware that they weren't alone. She turned to see Connor standing in the doorway.

At first, she thought her eyes might be deceiving her. Surely he wasn't really there, at that most inconvenient moment, his face looking as though it had been carved from granite.

But then he gave a big, bright smile and moved forward, greeting Natalie warmly. "Hey, Nat. It's good to see you. Been a long time, hasn't it? How's everything with you?"

"Connor!" Sharing a quick, oh-hell look with Mia, Natalie stood to exchange air kisses with her former coworker. "Great to see you. How's medical school? What brings you here today?"

"Medical school is going well, and I just stopped by to give this to Mia." He pulled an envelope from the inside pocket of his battered leather jacket. Because it wasn't an ICM day and he hadn't been required to wear a tie or his white coat, he'd dressed casually in a pullover, jeans and the jacket.

He looked very handsome, of course, as he always did. But his eyes...

Mia swallowed as she reached out for the envelope. If she'd had any optimism that he hadn't heard at least part of what Natalie had said before he'd entered the room, that hope died when she saw the turbulent expression in his unsmiling eyes. "What is this?"

"I was supposed to send this paperwork with Alexis to school today, but I forgot all about it this morning. It's a permission slip and some insurance information they need before the museum field trip on Friday. I wondered if you'd mind dropping it off when you pick her up today. I'd have run it by myself, but I'm on my way to James's place to study and the school is out of my way. Still, if it's too much trouble..."

"Of course it's no trouble," she assured him quickly. "Like you said, I'll be there, anyway."

"You're sure?"

"Absolutely." She tucked the envelope in her purse. "Have you had a chance to see anyone else here? I know Coach Johnson would like to see you."

"Tell him hello for me if you see him, okay? I'll try to stop by soon and catch up. But right now, I'm running late for the study session."

He turned to Natalie. "Great to see you, Nat. You and Mia should have a night out soon. Mia knows that I'm always available to watch Alexis when Mia has other plans."

"Yeah. We were just talking about that. Uh, see you around, Connor."

He nodded once and was gone.

Groaning loudly, Natalie sank back into her chair. "Can you believe he showed up here, out of the blue, at that very moment? Man, what were the odds? And why does that sort of thing always happen to me? At least he didn't act as though he heard what I said. That's a relief."

"Yeah. A relief," Mia muttered, though she knew very well that they hadn't been so fortunate.

What *were* the odds that he'd have walked in at that very minute? And how should she handle the fact that he had? Things had already been strained between them since those kisses in the power outage. They'd both pulled back again, expressing their tumultuous emotions only in occasional searching glances. They'd been careful not to touch, but when their hands had brushed by accident, they'd both jerked back as if they'd been shocked. The strain of pretending nothing had changed was beginning to show on them both.

It wasn't going to help things between them that he'd walked in on a conversation he never should have overheard. Should she act as though she was unaware that he'd heard anything at all? Try to explain, perhaps, or to assure him that Natalie had spoken out of turn, and risk making everything worse? Or should she simply accept that what Natalie had said struck much too close to the truth?

At that moment, Mia couldn't say with total confidence that her friend's accusations had been unjustified.

* * *

Still seething over the things he had heard Natalie say to Mia, Connor hoped he could put all his worries aside for a few hours to concentrate on his studies. The gross anatomy final was just over a week away and the thought of it filled him with apprehension. It would be an intense, comprehensive exam and it was going to require every bit of his concentration for him to do well. He couldn't help but resent that his relationship with Mia was becoming so complicated, so intrusive on his school work.

It wasn't her fault, he told himself as he rapped quickly on the door to James's apartment. She was obviously no happier about the developments than he was. He just wished he understood better what was going through her head.

Was Natalie right? Was Mia unhappy living with him? Did she really think he viewed her as an "unpaid housekeeper"?

"Hey, Connor. Come on in." James moved out of the doorway with an inviting wave of his hand.

Something about James's expression caught Connor's attention. "What's going on?"

"Just a minor meltdown," James replied in a murmur. "Haley's handling it."

Glancing toward the kitchen table where they usually studied, Connor saw that Anne was sniffling into a tissue while Haley hovered over her and Ron stood helplessly nearby, wringing his hands.

Connor groaned. Now what? "Is she okay?"

"She's worried about the test. She hasn't been getting enough sleep or eating right or giving herself any time to relax and unwind, and it all just caught up with her."

"What should we do?"

As clueless as Connor, James shrugged. "We follow Haley's lead, I guess. I think it takes another woman to understand this sort of thing."

His life had been so easy a year ago, Connor thought wearily, pushing a hand through his hair. He'd been surrounded by teenage athletes who responded, for the most part, to praise and threats and occasional bribes. His weekends had been filled with pickup basketball games and sports on TV.

He'd eaten when he felt like it, slept when he was tired, thought of tests only as something he administered to his own students. He'd had a group of casual friends to hang out with for fun and games. He and Mia had been the best of pals, able to ignore any simmering attraction and just enjoy being together, returning to their own safe quarters before any of those banked emotions could flare out of control. His future had been his own and any choices he'd made had affected no one other than himself.

Everything was different now. His life no longer felt like his own. He was tired, stressed, worried, frustrated, dejected and hopelessly in love with a woman who quite possibly viewed him and his sweet, needy daughter as obstacles to her own future plans.

And if he kept this up, he thought in self-disgust, he was going to sit next to Anne and burst into tears himself.

"Okay," he said loudly, moving forward in determination. "Let's make some coffee and break out the sweets. I know you've got cookies or cake or something around here, James. That housekeeper of yours always keeps your pantries stocked."

Everyone was looking at him in surprise now, even Anne, who'd lowered her tissue with one last sniffle.

"We're going to spend the next few hours guzzling caffeine and sugar and filling our heads with so many gross anatomy facts that there won't be any room left for thoughts of anything else," he stated firmly. "Anne, you know this information as well as anyone in this room. You're going to do fine. We all are. Now, let's get at it, okay?"

Anne drew a deep breath and tossed aside her tissue. "I need chocolate."

Connor smiled encouragingly. "That's the spirit. You got chocolate, James?"

Nodding in approval, James moved toward the fridge. "As a matter of fact, I do. Several kinds."

"Bring it on," Ron said, rubbing his hands together in anticipation. "Let's kick some gross anatomy butt."

Haley laughed and moved toward the coffeepot. "Works for me."

Rather pleased with himself, Connor tossed his backpack on the floor beside his usual seat at the table.

He just wished all his problems were so easily tackled.

That Saturday was Valentine's Day. No big deal, Mia assured herself as she served heart-shaped pancakes to Alexis. She'd declined another invitation for a double date with Natalie and Donnie and one of Donnie's many single buddies, preferring, instead, to spend the day taking Alexis for that long-promised outing at the zoo.

It was predicted to be a chilly but sunny afternoon, and they both needed the fresh air after the bad weather they'd been having lately had kept them cooped up in the house when they weren't at school. Mia figured they could bundle up in coats, scarves, hats and gloves and they'd be fine for a few hours outside. She would take her camera and she expected to get lots of cute shots of a pink-cheeked Alexis admiring the animals.

Connor wasn't up yet, but that didn't surprise her. She'd gotten up for a glass of water at three that morning and had noticed the light still on beneath his bedroom door. He needed every hour of sleep he would allow himself before the big exam, she thought with a disapproving shake of her head.

She had just filled Alexis's juice glass when Connor walked into the kitchen, almost hidden behind the gifts he carried. He handed Mia a dozen red roses in a beautiful glass vase. Before she could do more than murmur a surprised thank you, he turned to give Alexis a large white teddy bear that held a big red heart between its stuffed paws.

"Happy Valentine's Day," he said, looking at Alexis as he spoke, although Mia could tell he spoke to both of them. "Bet you thought I'd forget."

Alexis hugged the bear. "He's so soft. Thank you."

Mia buried her nose in the fragrant roses. He'd probably given them to her only because he'd gotten something for Alexis, but she was still pleased by the gesture. She loved fresh flowers, and roses were among her favorites. "They're beautiful. Thank you, Connor."

"I have something, too." Clutching the bear, Alexis dashed out of the room.

Mia turned to set the roses on the counter and picked up a small, gold box of chocolates she'd purchased on an impulse when she'd bought a little heart-shaped necklace for Alexis. She'd debated whether to get him anything, not wanting to risk any more mixed signals between them, but it seemed only polite to give him something. She'd figured candies were appropriate without being too ambiguous. And she knew he loved sweets. Eyeing the roses, she was glad she'd given in.

"I bought these for you," she said, turning to offer him the little box. "I thought you might like a few treats while you're studying."

His smile was just a little crooked, the expression in his eyes hard to read. "Thanks, Mia. I'll enjoy these."

"Here, Daddy." Alexis skipped back into the room bearing two large red hearts. "I made one for you and for Mia. We did them at school."

Accepting her gift, Mia smiled down at the heart bedecked with glued-on white doily, glitter and Alexis's carefully written "I love you, Mia." Her throat tight, she glanced at Connor's Valentine, which read "I love you, Daddy."

Even knowing the project had been directed by Alexis's perky teacher, Mia was deeply touched. She would treasure this little paper heart for the rest of her life, she thought as she knelt to kiss Alexis's soft cheek. "Thank you, sweetie. It's beautiful."

Already wearing her necklace with her pajamas, Alexis beamed. "You really like it?"

"I really do."

"And so do I." Connor's voice was just a bit husky when he leaned over to thank Alexis with his own cheek kiss. "It's the best Valentine I've ever gotten."

Bouncing on her toes, Alexis hugged her bear. "I like Valentine's Day."

"So do I," Connor said, straightening. And then his expression turned guilty. "I wish I could spend it with you both, but I'm afraid I have to go. I'm going to be working all day in the lab."

"That's okay," Mia assured him. "You need to prepare for your final. Alexis and I have plans for this afternoon, so we'll get along fine."

"I'm sure you will," he murmured, holding her gaze for just a moment. And then he looked at Alexis. "I might be late getting in tonight. You two have a great day, okay? And thanks again for the gifts."

Still holding the paper heart from his daughter, Mia watched with a dull ache in her chest as he turned and left the room.

Connor could feel the pressure building inside him as each day passed that week. His study group had been putting in long, intense hours preparing for the gross anatomy final while trying to keep up with their other classes. He'd studied with them, with his gross anatomy lab partners, on his own in the library and coffee shops and locked in his room late at night. He'd eaten when he'd remembered, slept in exhausted snatches and walked around in a fog of medical and scientific facts, trying to commit them all to memory.

He didn't want to question too closely if part of his obsession with schoolwork was to keep him from thinking too much about Mia. If studying at night kept him from thinking about her lying in her own bed only a few yards from his bedroom. Kept him from reliving the feel of heated kisses and soft curves pressed against him.

He might be focused on his education, but he was still a healthy, relatively young male with needs, he thought irritably. The woman he wanted—the woman he loved—was living in the same house with him, doing everything she could to make his life easier. Yet it only seemed to become more complicated the more time he spent with her.

He wasn't sure how much longer he could go on this way.

More than once during that week he let his thoughts drift back to those easier times a year earlier. And he wondered if he had failed to properly appreciate those carefree, footloose days.

He didn't know what he would have done without his study group to support him. They, more than anyone in the world, could understand some of what he was going through, because they were faced with similar difficulties in their own lives. Trying to balance the stress of school with the demands of family and other personal responsibilities.

It wasn't an easy task, which was why medical students were regularly treated to speeches and workshops about dealing with stress and depression without turning to drugs or alcohol or thoughts of quitting or even suicide. Only that week, they'd been informed that a recent study had suggested that as many as eleven percent of all medical students contemplated that ultimate escape during the first two years of training.

While Connor thought he was dealing with the pressure better than that, he certainly understood how despair and panic could set in, especially for students who were struggling and who hadn't found the emotional support he'd lucked into with his increasingly close-knit study group. And, he admitted, with

Mia. Despite his complicated and frustrating feelings for her, he couldn't have gotten by during the past months without her to take care of Alexis. And him, for that matter. She quietly cooked and cleaned and did laundry and dealt with the day-to-day issues that had freed him to concentrate on his studies…and he had given her damned little in return.

Guilt swamped him, adding to the weight on his shoulders. After this test, he vowed, he was going to somehow find a way to do more of his share around the house.

On Thursday night he sat at the kitchen table, having decided to study at home that evening because of the thunderstorm raging outside. Lightning flashed outside and booms of thunder rattled the windows, interfering with his concentration, but he forced himself to keep his eyes on the material.

February had certainly been a turbulent month, weather-wise, he thought with a deep sigh. Not to mention his personal life.

Mia was keeping Alexis entertained and diverted from the storm. They were playing games back in Alexis's room. Connor could hear their voices drifting toward him between claps of thunder. Maybe because of the storm, Alexis seemed to be uncharacteristically wound up. She was talking more loudly, laughing more shrilly than usual. Twice she dashed through the living room and into the kitchen for drinks of water, followed by Mia, who looked apologetically at Connor and admonished Alexis to settle down a little.

A hard gust of wind made the house creak around him. He hoped the storm didn't cause any damage to the house or the roof. Lightning flashed through the windows, followed by a clap of thunder so loud that Connor could almost hear his ears ring. Alexis squealed in the back, followed by soothing words from Mia. He couldn't hear what she said, but her tone was obviously intended to reassure the child.

He could feel the tension knotting the muscles in his neck and shoulders. Between the storm and his housemates, he was finding it harder and harder to concentrate. Maybe he should have studied in the library that evening, but then he'd have felt guilty leaving Mia to deal with the storm and any potential damage on her own.

Fortunately, the storm had abated somewhat by Alexis's bedtime. Rain still pounded the roof, but the lightning had moved farther away, leaving only a low rumble of thunder in its wake.

"I'm going to bed now, Daddy." Alexis darted into the kitchen with her Valentine bear—now named Bob, for some reason—clutched in one arm and Pete dangling over her other arm. "Good night. Oof—"

She'd been running toward him, and her feet had slipped on the glossy wooden floor. She made hard contact with the table where he sat, knocking his laptop computer off the edge, scattering books and papers all around them.

"Darn it, Alexis!" Connor made a frantic grab for his computer, catching it just before it crashed to the floor.

That could have been a disaster, he thought with a gulp. He didn't even want to think about losing all his files, trying to replace his computer and reload everything less than a week before his final exam. "Now I've got to try to get all this stuff back in order. How many times has Mia told you not to run in the house?"

Setting the computer carefully back on the table, he frowned at Alexis, then swallowed a groan.

Her big navy eyes had filled with tears that were already leaking down her cheeks. "I'm sorry," she whispered. "It was an accident."

He drew a deep breath, struggling for patience.

"I know it was an accident," he said, trying to use a more gentle tone. "But you still have to be more careful. You could have broken something. Or even worse, you could have been hurt yourself. There's a reason Mia tells you not to run inside."

"Okay." Subdued, she hung her head. "Good night."

"Good night, princess. Sleep well, okay?" He gave her an

awkward hug that she didn't return, then watched as she shuffled away.

Mia stood in the doorway, her expression solemn. She placed a hand on Alexis's shoulder and turned to walk her toward the bedrooms, leaving Connor cursing beneath his breath.

Great, he thought savagely. He'd yelled at his kid and made her cry. They probably both hated him now.

He really should have studied at the library.

Mia stood quietly in the doorway to the kitchen a little while later, watching Connor as he shuffled and stacked papers and arranged open textbooks. He didn't know she was there, so she had a moment to study him. His jaw was set, his shoulders tensed. He looked tired and frustrated and dejected.

As if he'd suddenly sensed her standing there, he looked around, meeting her eyes with a stormy expression in his own. "She's not still crying, is she?"

"No. She's already sound asleep. I assured her you weren't really angry with her, and then I stayed with her until she fell asleep, which didn't take long. She was tired. And she knows, by the way, that she shouldn't have been running in the house. She promised she wouldn't do so again—although I expect she'll forget again, eventually."

A muscle rippled in his jaw as he swallowed. "I shouldn't have yelled at her."

She gave a little shrug and moved toward him. "It probably won't be the last time. My dad chewed me out a few times when I misbehaved, and I turned out well enough."

"Yeah, but your circumstances were different. You weren't still just getting to know him at Alexis's age."

He really was beating himself up about this. Stopping beside his chair, she rested a hand on his taut shoulder. "It's okay, Connor. I promise you, Alexis has not been permanently traumatized. Is your computer okay?"

"Yeah. I caught it before it hit the floor."

"Is there anything I can do to help you put your things back in order? Or maybe to help you study? I'd be happy to quiz you for a while if it would help."

She was relieved to see his expression lighten a little now that she'd given him some reassurance. Had he really expected her to be angry with him for snapping at Alexis? That was the impression she'd gotten when he'd first spotted her standing there.

She had to admit that she hadn't liked seeing the child's tears and had inwardly cringed during the brief incident, and maybe she thought he could have handled it a little better, but she figured he was angry enough with himself. There was no need for her to ladle on the guilt. Alexis really shouldn't have been running through the house. As Connor had pointed out, and Mia had reiterated afterward, rules were made for a reason. They had to enforce them now or risk having Alexis turn into an out-of-control adolescent later.

"I think I'm going to take a break for a few minutes before getting back to it," Connor said, pushing himself out of his chair. "I need to stretch."

Dropping her hand to her side, she moved a step back. "Do you want something to eat? A cup of tea, maybe?"

"No, I'm okay for now. I just—"

He stumbled when his foot slid on a pencil that had fallen unnoticed to the floor. Steadying himself quickly, he shook his head and bent to pick it up at the same time Mia reached down for it. They bumped heads, laughed, reached again for the pencil in unison, then bumped into each other again.

"I'll get it," Connor said, catching her shoulders to keep her from losing her balance with the second collision. "Before we end up—"

His teasing words faded into silence.

They knelt very close together, their knees touching, his hands on her forearms. Distant lightning strobed against the kitchen window and a low rumble of thunder echoed the sudden pounding of Mia's heart.

"Damn it," Connor muttered, his fingers tightening on her arms.

Hardly romantic words, but his tormented tone made her throat tighten. Without giving herself a moment to think, she leaned toward him, wrapped her arms around his knotted shoulders and pressed her mouth to his.

Chapter Eleven

Connor closed his bedroom door very quietly and pressed the lock. They hadn't turned on a light, but there was just enough illumination in the shadowy room for her to see the tumultuous play of emotions across his face. "Mia—"

"Shh." She pressed her fingertips against his lips and moved closer.

He was so tense. The tendons in his arms and thighs were as rigid as granite. His desire for her was obvious when she fitted herself fluidly against him. Her pulse raced with an answering hunger she could no longer deny.

He held himself back for a moment, his muscles quivering with the effort. She suspected that he was struggling to think, trying to stay in control, but she smothered his mouth beneath hers before he could voice his reservations. She didn't want to think. Didn't want to worry or dread or anticipate. For this one night, she wanted only to feel. To offer what he needed and take what she wanted. To finally give in to what had been building between them for longer than either had been willing to admit.

She felt the moment Connor stopped trying to resist. A hard breath jolted through him and he dragged her closer, his mouth closing over hers with an almost desperate intensity. His tongue plunged between her lips and she welcomed him eagerly, savoring the spicy taste of him. He lifted her onto her tiptoes and she wrapped her arms around his neck, trying to get closer to him even though they were already plastered together.

Mindful of the need for quiet, they fell onto the bed, their gasps and moans hushed but still heartfelt. Clothes fell heedlessly aside. Connor groped in the nightstand drawer with one hand while ridding himself of his jeans with the other. He didn't even bother to close the drawer when he rushed back to her, rolling with her on the tumbled bedclothes.

They moved together as if they'd been lovers forever. And yet it was still so much different than Mia had ever imagined. So much more than she had even hoped.

She had never felt like this before. Shuddering in his arms, she heard the cliché echo through her head, and she would have winced at her own triteness had she had the strength to do anything but lie there and gasp for air. But it was true, nonetheless. Nothing had ever felt this good. This…right.

His skin hot and damp, his breathing labored, Connor lay beside her, holding her tightly against his side. She heard him swallow, heard him start to say something, but then he fell silent again, as if he weren't yet up to the effort of speech.

Feeling much the same way, she nestled her cheek into his shoulder, her hand resting on his flat stomach. Doubts and uncertainties were beginning to whisper at the back of her mind, but she pushed them away. She would deal with them later, she promised herself. She'd have no other choice, eventually. But she could allow herself to appreciate this intimate warmth for a few more lovely moments.

Connor's lips moved against her forehead. "I should get back to studying," he murmured, his voice low, still a little rough-edged.

"You need some rest."

"I couldn't sleep now, anyway. I guess you could say I've been reinvigorated. Thanks."

She smiled and lifted her head to look at him. "Glad I could help."

Laughing softly, he snagged the back of her head and pulled her for another kiss, this one more gentle and lingering than the ones they had exchanged in the heat of passion.

His smile was gone by the time the kiss ended. "We'll have to talk about this, you know."

She swallowed, feeling euphoria slip away despite her best efforts to hold on to it. "I know. But maybe now isn't the best time."

"No. But soon."

"Yes."

Sighing, he rolled away from her, reaching for his clothes. "My robe is on the end of the bed—er, no, I guess it's on the floor now. You can wear it to go back to your room."

Nodding, she fumbled for the soft terry robe, then wrapped it around herself. She studied Connor through her lashes as she gathered her own tangled garments. Although she couldn't completely interpret his expression, he definitely looked more relaxed. Completely alert. She suspected that he would be able to concentrate fully on his studying now.

She supposed she should be pleased about that. After all, she'd wanted to help him relax, right?

He tugged his shirt over his head. "You can go on to bed, if you're tired. I'll put out the lights and check the locks when I'm ready to turn in."

She could take a hint. Even though it was a full hour earlier than she usually went to bed, she nodded. "I am a little tired.

You're sure there's nothing I can do to help you study tonight? Because I'd be happy to—"

He interrupted by dropping a light kiss on her forehead. "Thanks, but I'll do better tackling it on my own tonight."

"Okay, then. Good night, Connor."

He was already moving toward the door. In a hurry to get back to his studying...or running away from the emotions that had sprung up between them? Maybe a combination of both, she decided, following more slowly.

He turned to her in the doorway, after glancing down the hall to make sure all was still quiet from his daughter's room.

"Mia," he said, his voice very low. "I'm sure you already know this, but I—"

She held her breath when he hesitated, her heart beating rapidly in her throat.

"I'd be completely lost without you," he finished after a moment. "I just want you to know how much I appreciate you."

She forced a smile. "Go study, Connor. And then try to get some sleep. I'll see you tomorrow."

"Yeah, okay. Good night."

"Good night," she whispered, then headed wearily toward her room as he moved off in the other direction.

Connor overslept Friday morning. No big surprise because he hadn't gone to bed until almost 3 a.m.

Surprisingly enough, he thought as he showered quickly and threw on his clothes, he'd actually been able to study during those quiet nighttime hours. He would have expected to be distracted by thoughts of Mia, by second thoughts and misgivings, or at the very least by leisurely mental replays. Instead, his mind had been clear and focused, his mood almost light as he'd gone over material that seemed oddly uncomplicated in those hours.

He was such a guy, he thought with a wry shake of his head. He'd been revitalized by the oldest method on record. Amazing what a round of hot, great sex could do for a man after a long, dry spell of going without.

But it was more than that, he told himself as he threw his things into his car and started the engine. He hadn't wanted to be with just any woman. He'd wanted Mia. Wanted her so badly he hadn't been able to concentrate fully on anything else for days. Weeks.

He didn't know what the future held for him and he didn't have time to dwell on it at the moment, but as he drove toward the campus, he felt more optimistic than he had in some time. Once he got past this final, he promised himself, he and Mia would have a long-overdue talk.

He was working with his study group in James's apartment when his cell phone rang later that afternoon. Seeing Mia's number on the screen, he moved across the room to take the call. "Mia? Is everything okay?"

"Yes, it's fine. I hope I'm not interrupting anything…"

"I can take a minute. What's up?"

"If it's okay with you, I'd like to take Alexis to my family's house on Lake Catherine this weekend. They're all gathering there for my dad's birthday, which is Sunday. I'd planned to take her for a few hours Sunday, but I think she'd enjoy staying the weekend to play with Nicklaus and Caroline."

He frowned in response to what sounded like an odd tone in her voice. Was she a little self-conscious about what had happened between them last night? Understandable, of course, but for some reason, he thought there was more to it. "Sure. Of course. When are you leaving?"

"In about an hour, I guess. As soon as I can get our things together. We'll be home Sunday afternoon."

"Oh. I see."

"It's probably best for you, anyway. After all, you have that big test Monday and it will be easier for you to study without us there to bother you."

"You know I like having you both there."

"I know. But there will still be fewer interruptions without us. I'll have my cell with me, of course, if you need anything."

"I'll be fine." She hadn't even mentioned this weekend trip before, he thought with a frown. Had it been something she'd considered earlier—or was she jumping on the excuse to run because of last night? "Have a good time."

"We will. Thanks. And good luck with your studies."

Slipping the phone back into its holder on his belt, he turned somberly back to the group gathered around James's table. His good mood of earlier had just taken a sharp turn back into doubt and insecurity.

Was Mia having regrets today? She'd certainly been fully involved last night, but maybe she was having second thoughts now that she'd had time to think about their actions. Maybe she was afraid that too much had changed between them now, and not necessarily for the better.

"Is everything okay at home, Connor?" Haley asked, looking up at him in concern.

He spread his hands and answered with complete honesty. "I don't have the faintest clue."

Ron shook his head in sympathy. "Dude. Glad I'm not in your shoes."

Haley punched his arm. "Ron!"

"Ow. I'm just saying—"

With a wry smile, Connor slid into his seat. "Let's just get back to work, okay? Everything will work out for the best somehow."

He had to keep telling himself that in an effort to make himself believe it.

He studied late into the night Saturday. Because no one was there to disturb, he kept all the lights burning in his house and made no effort to be quiet when he rambled around in the kitchen for snacks and drinks. As it was a little cool in the house, he wore a ragged sweatshirt and fleece pants, but he could be studying in his underwear, if he wanted to, he thought with a wry smile. After all, no one was there to see him.

Leaving dirty dishes in the sink to put away later, he carried a cold can of soda to the table where he was studying. He looked around the empty room for a moment while he took his first sip. Several times during the past few weeks he had remembered what it was like to be on his own, responsible for no one but himself. If he ignored the doll peeking out from a sofa cushion and a coffee mug sitting by the coffeemaker with Mia's name printed on it, he could almost imagine that he had gone back in time to those solitary bachelor days.

Shaking his head, he reached for a notebook, then frowned when he realized it wasn't where he'd thought. He must have left it in his room.

Grumbling, he wandered through the living room and down the hallway to his bedroom. He found the notebook on his desk. He looked at his bed on his way out of the room. Would he ever see that bed again without remembering Mia in his arms there? Without wanting to be with her there again?

Turning abruptly, he left the room, then paused again, his gaze turning toward the two bedrooms at the other end of the short hallway. Both doors were open and the rooms beyond were dark. Empty. The silence settled heavily around him and for the first time in his memory, he felt lonely in the little house he'd once considered a cozy refuge.

What if he could go back in time, to those earlier, easier days? What if some quirk of magic or fate gave him that option? Would he choose to place himself on a basketball court with his buddies a year earlier, laughing like an idiot and having nothing waiting for him after the game but a takeout and a stack of papers to grade? Back when Mia had been a comfortable friend to call for a shared movie or pizza and neither of them had worried overly much about their future? Back before anyone had ever called him "Daddy" and expected him to provide shelter and guidance and security?

Would he go back if he could? The mental question seemed to echo in the hushed shadows around him, as if the house itself waited for his answer.

He gave a hard shake of his head and moved toward the kitchen, back to the lecture notes that awaited him. Stress and lack of sleep must be getting to him. It wasn't like him to be so foolish and fanciful.

"It is what it is," he muttered, plopping down into his chair again. No going back. No rewriting reality.

Yet even as he opened his book, he knew there was no real doubt what his answer would have been had he been given that impossible choice.

He wouldn't go back.

Mia found a note from Connor in the kitchen when she and Alexis returned from the weekend at the lake house her family had owned since Mia was a teenager. He would be studying in the lab and with his group until late, the note said. Don't wait up for him.

Alexis looked disappointed and Mia knew the feeling. "You'll see him tomorrow. If not in the morning, then after school. His big test will be over then and he'll have time for you to tell him all about your weekend with Nicklaus and Caroline."

"Okay."

"Go put away your things and I'll make us some dinner. You'll want to take your bath and get in bed on time tonight because you were up late last night."

Alexis and Mia's niece and nephew had lain awake until almost ten giggling and chattering in the two sets of bunk beds set up in what the family referred to as the kids' room. There were four bedrooms in the rambling cottage, all surrounding a large great room that served as living room and dining room with an open, attached kitchen.

The weekend had been noisy and active and a little chaotic with five adults and three children in the house, playing games, watching sports, taking hikes along the water's edge and through the nearby woods in the crisp, cool air. It had been exactly what Mia needed. A few days packed too busy for worrying and stewing, surrounded by people who loved her unconditionally and expected nothing from her but love in return.

She turned in early that night. Partially because she was tired, but maybe as a way to avoid facing Connor for a few more hours. She didn't fall instantly asleep, but lay in her bed, staring at the ceiling until she heard him arrive home just before midnight.

She heard his footsteps through the kitchen and the living room. Held her breath as she heard him pause in the hallway. Was he looking at her door? She could almost sense him out there, gazing her way.

But then she heard him walk into his own room and close his door. She released her breath in a low sigh.

They couldn't go on like this, of course. She couldn't continue to avoid him. Eventually—soon—she was going to have to face him again for the first time since she had left his bed last week. And she was going to have to decide exactly how they would continue from here.

Connor looked exhausted when he arrived home late Monday afternoon, but Mia could tell by her first look at him that he was satisfied with his performance on the gross anatomy final.

"You did well?" she asked when he walked in.

He gave her a tired smile. "I think so. It was as hard as I expected, but I was pretty confident with my answers."

"That's great. I know you're glad to have that class behind you."

He nodded vigorously. "Very much so. Definitely the most difficult class I've ever taken in my life. But I got through it."

She smiled. "I hope you're hungry. I made lasagna."

His eyes lit up. "Lasagna? My favorite meal."

"I know that. And we're having chocolate chess pie for dessert. To celebrate your survival of the class."

"My favorite meal and my favorite dessert. Mia, you're an angel."

Her heart twisted a little, but she smiled and waved him away. "Go wash up. I'll get the food on the table."

He hesitated a moment, as though he wanted to say—or do—something more. His gaze focused on her mouth, and she wondered if he was thinking about kissing her. Her own lips tingled in anticipation.

"Daddy! You're home. I want to tell you what I did at the lake house." Alexis was practically bouncing as she came into the kitchen. Not running, Mia noted with a faint smile, but definitely hurrying.

Connor swept Alexis into a hug. "Hi, princess. I want to hear all about your weekend. Just let me go wash my hands, okay? You can tell me all about it during the delicious dinner Mia has made for us."

Torn between relief and disappointment, Mia turned back to her dinner preparations. "Alexis, would you like to put the napkins on the table?" she asked lightly.

There was no opportunity for Mia and Connor to talk during dinner. Alexis kept up a cheery monologue, barely taking time to chew and swallow before thinking of another tidbit to share with her father about her weekend with Mia's family. Connor listened intently, smiling, laughing when appropriate, asking questions and encouraging her to continue.

Watching the two of them together, Mia was struck by how much more easily they communicated than they had at the start. Alexis seemed more comfortable with her father now, and he was more relaxed with her in return. There was no question that the child was still partial to Mia, but her affections were becoming just a bit more balanced. Maybe this summer, when Alexis was out of school and Connor had a little more free time, the two of them could find things to do, just the two of them. Father-daughter outings. Family things.

"This meal is great, Mia. You outdid yourself tonight."

She smiled a bit too brightly. "I'm glad you like it. You're saving room for dessert, aren't you?"

"Are you kidding? You couldn't stop me from having some of that pie." He looked at Alexis. "I tasted Mia's chocolate chess pie for the first time not long after she and I met. That's when I knew we were going to be best friends forever."

Alexis giggled. "Because of her pie?"

"Well, maybe her lasagna had something to do with it, too."

Grinning, the child glanced toward Mia. "I think Daddy likes your cooking."

"Yes, I think he does, too." She reached abruptly for her glass. "I'd like some more tea. Anyone else need anything while I'm up?"

They both assured her they were fine. They were already talking again as Mia opened the refrigerator door and took out the tea pitcher.

Connor insisted on cleaning up after the meal. It was the least he could do, he argued, after Mia had gone to so much trouble. Besides, with her habit of cleaning as she cooked, it wasn't as if there was much left for him to do, he added.

She spent the next hour helping Alexis with a reading assignment and then getting her ready for bed. When the child was bathed and tucked snugly into bed, Mia gathered her courage and went to rejoin Connor in the living room, resisting a cowardly impulse to hide in her own room.

Connor was sprawled in his easy chair, reading a medical textbook, when Mia walked in. He looked up with a slightly distracted smile. "Is she asleep?"

"If not, she's almost there. Her eyes were closing when I left her."

He set his book aside and stretched. "I told myself I was going to take an evening off from studying, but it's hard to make myself do so. I keep remembering that I still have three more classes to complete this semester."

"You deserve a few hours just to unwind after that test. Can I get you anything?"

He groaned and waved her toward the couch. "Sit down. I've had plenty to eat and drink. Let's just relax for now, okay?"

Sinking into the cushions, she nodded. "I have a little paperwork to do for school tomorrow, but it'll only take me twenty minutes or so. I can chat a while."

A fleeting frown crossed his face, as if chatting wasn't exactly what he'd had in mind, but he nodded equably. "I've heard all about Alexis's weekend. How about you? Did you have a nice time with your family?"

"Very nice, thanks. We played lots of board games, took some walks, had a birthday party for Dad. Ate a lot," she added with a slight grimace.

"It sounds nice."

"It was."

"Alexis is crazy about your family. She's obviously adopted them for her own."

"They feel the same way about her. Nicklaus and Caroline love spending time with her, and my parents think she's adorable. Probably because she is," she added with a little laugh.

"She hasn't had any more nightmares lately?"

"No. I hope that phase is over."

"Yeah, so do I."

Mia twisted her fingers in her lap, knowing the small talk was about to end. She tried to delay the inevitable just a bit longer. "How do you think your study group did on the exam?"

"James pretty much aced it, I'm sure, as did Anne, though she'll probably fret about it until the grades are posted. Haley seemed well prepared, so I'm sure she did okay. Ron—"

He shrugged. "It's hard to tell with Ron. He works hard, but he doesn't seem to take anything too seriously. Even if he blew it, I'm not sure the rest of us would ever know."

"You've become quite close with them, haven't you?"

"Yeah, I guess I have. They're great people."

"You don't get to see your old friends much these days."

"I know," he admitted with a wince. "I hate that, but I've just had so little extra time. Besides which, we don't seem to have as much in common these days. It was playing sports that drew us together mostly, and I don't have as much opportunity for that these days, especially since Alexis arrived. And they like to hang out in the bars afterward, drinking beer and picking up women, and that's not really my thing anymore. Again, part of that is due to Alexis—I mean, I'm a father now, you know? I should act like one."

In other words, his life was changing. He was slowly leaving his old life behind. His new friends had more in common with him, knew exactly what it was like to go through medical school, and the shared experiences drew them closer together. Whatever energy he had left was rightly given to his daughter.

So what did that leave for her? A few moments of attention on the odd evening away from his studies, like tonight?

She moistened her lips and clenched her hands more tightly together.

After a moment, Connor pushed a hand through his hair and leaned forward in his chair, his eyes focused on her face. "We seem to be going out of our way to avoid the one topic we should probably be discussing."

She glanced down at her white-knuckled fingers. "I know."

"What happened between us the other night—"

"—was amazing," she cut in quickly. "I don't regret it."

After a slight pause, he prodded, "But...?"

"But I think we should slow down again," she finished in a rush. "Everything is still in transition here. We still have to think about Alexis, and you have your classes to finish. I've got midterm exams coming up, then all the hectic, end-of-the-year stuff. And—"

He held up a hand, his face inscrutable. "Okay, I get the message."

"No regrets," she repeated in case he'd missed that part. "It's just…well, it's just the wrong time for us to start anything that has the potential to cause so many problems in the long run."

"I'm sure you're right. As always."

There was just enough sting in his words to make her wince. "Connor—"

He held up both hands this time. "No, Mia. I'm sorry. You really are right. It's the worst possible time for me. For both of us."

"Oh." Her heart sank a little even as she told herself she was glad he was being rational about this. "Well—"

"I know you've had a lot to deal with the last few months," he added. "It's pretty well all been on your shoulders to keep the house going and take care of Alexis and keep up with your own work. Natalie was right about that."

She grimaced. "No, she wasn't. I'm sorry you heard what she said, but she didn't know what she was talking about."

"Of course she did. She's your friend and she cares about you. She wants what's best for you. As do I."

Not sure where this was headed now, she tilted her head and studied him with a frown. "Um—"

"I'm going to start doing more around here," he announced firmly. "I'll still have to study, but I can do more of it at home so I can help you out a little more. If nothing else, I can do laundry while I study. Just takes a few minutes to throw in a load of clothes or fold some towels. I can certainly manage that."

Surely he didn't think her biggest concern was the division of household labor. "There's no need for that. I said all along that we'd consider child care and housework my way of paying rent."

He shook his head. "You've been doing too much. And

you've done it all without a word of complaint. The least I can do to repay you for all your help is to pitch in a bit more."

Repay her. The words sank heavily into her heart.

She had never wanted his gratitude. And she certainly didn't want him to feel that he owed her anything. If he couldn't understand that...

If he couldn't understand that, then there wasn't a chance that he could offer her what she really needed from him, she thought sadly.

He reached for his textbook. "Maybe I will read another chapter tonight. You said something about having some paperwork to do before tomorrow?"

Nodding numbly, she stood. "I'll go do that now. I— Good night, Connor."

"Good night, Mia," he answered without looking up from his book.

Swallowing hard, she turned to leave the room, crossing her arms against a sudden chill.

By the middle of March, Mia had convinced herself that she and Connor had done absolutely the right thing in drawing back from an intimate relationship. They were both very busy during those two weeks.

As Connor has promised, he made more of an effort to help out around the house, sharing responsibilities for Alexis to give Mia more time for her spring duties at school. He still spent quite a few hours with his study group, of course, but he always made sure to ask if Mia needed him at home before he made plans with them. He started bringing home takeout once a week, so she didn't have to cook, and he followed through on his promise to do laundry while he studied at the kitchen table. There were times when he was almost too helpful, getting underfoot and unintentionally interfering with the efficient routines she had established since moving in.

They were very polite, cheerfully friendly, scrupulously cooperative. Still friends, Mia thought with a fleeting sadness, if not the very best of friends anymore.

If Alexis noticed any difference, it wasn't obvious. She continued to enjoy her school, her friends, her dance classes. She still entertained herself very well with her dolls and art supplies and enjoyed playing the video game with Connor whenever he could spare an hour. Duncan made an occasional appearance, always bearing gifts, and Alexis thrived on those visits from her pop. She still spoke occasionally of her life back in Springfield, but those memories seemed to be growing hazy for her. Mia thought it was mostly because she was so young that the child had adapted so easily to her new life.

Mia wouldn't say that she, herself, was happy during those two weeks. But at least she was protecting herself from future heartbreak, she rationalized. Refusing to allow herself to get caught up in fantasy and foolish hope. That was the wisest course for her to take. Right?

So why was she so painfully empty whenever she stopped running long enough just to let herself feel?

It was another rainy Saturday afternoon, and Mia was mopping the kitchen floor when Connor came in. He stopped with a comical overbalance to keep himself from stepping on the wet tiles. "Oh. Sorry. Didn't know you were mopping."

"It's okay. You can walk across it."

She smiled a little as he made his way across the floor with exaggerated tiptoes, setting down as little of his feet as possible. "Where's Alexis?" he asked, when he made it safely to the wood floor of the living room.

"She's still at the dance school party. Connie's bringing her home afterward. She should be home in about an hour."

"Oh, yeah. I forgot about the party." He pushed a hand through his hair. "Anything I can do to help you?"

"No, I'm finished." She set the mop in the laundry room. She wore a soft pair of slippers with her jeans and green, V-neck T-shirt, so she didn't worry about crossing the damp floor. "How did your study session go today?"

"Pretty well, I think. We got through all the lecture notes from the past week, so we're caught up for Monday."

"That's good. You got a couple of things from the school in today's mail. I set them on the table."

"Okay, thanks."

She'd left a half-finished can of soda sitting on a coaster on the coffee table. She picked it up and took a long swig of the drink that was getting a little warm and flat. She was thirsty enough that it tasted good anyway.

Connor flipped through his mail, then turned to her with a hand at the back of his neck. "You're sure there's nothing I can do? Laundry? Run the vacuum, maybe?"

"You did all the laundry yesterday and I've already run the vacuum. All I plan to do now is sweep the front porch and then I—"

"I can do that," he said, moving in that direction.

"Connor, would you stop?" she asked, two weeks of pent-up emotion exploding out of her. "I get it, you're trying to help around the house more. But to be perfectly frank, you're getting on my nerves."

He stumbled to a halt. "What is that supposed to mean?"

"Exactly what I said. I don't need you to go to such extremes to make things easier for me here. I was taking care of the house perfectly well before you decided you had to 'repay' me for my efforts."

Apparently she wasn't the only one in whom frustration had been building. He planted his fists on his hips and scowled at her with utter male exasperation. "What the hell do you expect from me? Am I doing too little or too much around here? Are we friends or roommates or more? Damn it, I need you to tell me what you want."

"What I want is for you to—" She swallowed the words with a muttered curse when the front doorbell jangled stridently to interrupt her.

"I'll see who that is," she snapped, turning. "But you and I are going to have to finish this."

"Damn straight we are," he muttered, crossing his arms with a mulish expression.

She opened the door without checking to see who stood on the other side, then reached out quickly to unlock the storm door. Her heart began to pound in dread. "Paul? What's wrong? What's happened?"

Her brother reached out to catch her arm, his grave expression leaving no doubt that he hadn't brought good news. "I came to get you. Dad's had a heart attack. He's in the hospital in Hot Springs. Mom wants you to come."

Her own chest ached so much that it was hard to draw a breath. Dazed, she turned to Connor. "I—"

Connor was already moving toward her, concern for her softening his eyes. "Go throw some clothes in a bag," he said gently. "Is there anything I can do?"

"I don't— Alexis—"

"Alexis will be fine," he assured her. "Go be with your family."

It took her less than fifteen minutes to pack. She wasn't even sure what she'd grabbed out of her closet, but she thought she had enough to get by for a few days. Paul was waiting impatiently when she returned to the living room. He grabbed her bag and told her he'd be in the car.

"I'll just get my purse. Two minutes," Mia promised unsteadily.

Her brother nodded, shook Connor's hand, then let himself out.

Connor handed Mia her purse. "Your cell phone was on the counter. I stuck it in the pocket inside your bag."

"Thank you. Are you sure—"

"I'm sure we'll be fine," he promised, smoothing her hair

away from her face with one hand as he gazed down at her. "I hope everything is okay with your dad, Mia."

She swallowed hard and whispered, "So do I."

He brushed his lips across hers. "Call me if there's anything I can do."

Clutching his shirt, she leaned against him for a moment, wishing futilely that he could go with her. And then she turned away with a low moan and hurried toward the door.

Chapter Twelve

It was the longest week of Mia's life. Her father had surgery on Sunday and after that, developed a fever that scared them all. Mia's mother didn't handle the situation well, becoming almost paralyzed by fear and dread. She clung to her children and Mia rarely left her mother's side.

As concerned as she was with her parents, Mia also worried endlessly about how Connor and Alexis were getting along. A substitute teacher was handling her duties at the school, but she'd had no one to fill in for her at home.

Connor called her often for updates and to offer his assistance in any way she needed, but when she asked how things were at home, he would answer only with blithe assurances that everything was under control. She knew he wouldn't tell her differently no matter how bad it was there, because he wouldn't want to add to her worries. She paced the hospital hallways, her mind filled with dire thoughts about her father's prognosis and about everything that could be going wrong at home.

During the few hours when she was able to sleep, she kept waking up, instinctively listening for Alexis before realizing where she was. After only these few months, Alexis had become so much a part of her life, a part of her heart, that she could hardly imagine life without her now.

As for Connor…she missed him so badly that she ached. So many times she wished she had his strong arms around her during those tortuous days. His phone calls cheered her and bolstered her. She had no doubt that all she had to do was say the word and he would drop everything and come to her.

That knowledge gave her strength. She didn't really have the time nor the energy to dwell on her relationship with Connor during those days, but at the back of her mind she knew that she would have to reassess once this was all over and her dad was safely home again on his way to recovery. She refused to consider any other possible outcome.

Four nights after Mia had left, Connor was jerked out of his studying by a cry from Alexis's room. It was after eleven and she'd been in bed for hours. He hurried to her, figuring she'd had another nightmare.

"Mia!"

Alexis was sitting up in her bed, her eyes open but unfocused, her chin quivering. He wasn't sure if she was awake or still mostly asleep, so he approached quietly, his tone soothing. "What's wrong, Alexis?"

"Where's Mia?" she asked in a tearful mumble.

He bit back a groan, hoping this wasn't going to turn into a sob-fest. He wasn't sure he would be able to comfort her if she had her heart set on Mia's administrations.

He tried to speak calmly, bracingly. "Mia's visiting her parents, remember? But I'm here. Did you have another bad dream?"

She nodded tearfully. "I miss Mia."

"I know, princess. She'll be home in a few days. And, uh,

she'll be very proud of you for being such a big girl while she's gone," he added, hoping that would encourage her.

Letting that soak in for a moment, she glanced around uncertainly. "I think I heard something under my bed."

Was she trying to think of a way to detain him longer? Reaching the conclusion that she was only partially awake, and telling himself this was a normal part of childhood—he'd imagined a few monsters in the closet in his own boyhood—Connor tried to remember how his parents had handled this sort of thing. "You were only dreaming, Alexis. There's nothing under your bed. Do you want me to look and make sure?"

She drew in a halting breath and nodded. She gathered her stuffed cat and her Valentine bear into her arms, then peered over their heads as Connor obligingly went down on his knees and looked under the bed. Just to reassure her, he also checked the closet.

"Not a thing in here to bother you," he concluded heartily. "And I'll be in the living room just a shout away, okay? If you need anything at all, just say my name and I'll be here in half a second flat."

Allowing him to settle her back down against the pillows, she asked, "You won't go anywhere?"

"No, Alexis, I won't go anywhere," he promised, leaning over to kiss her forehead. "You're my little girl and I love you. I'm going to take care of you and keep you safe, okay?"

She snuggled against her stuffed friends and nodded, her eyelids already closing again. "'Night, Daddy."

He stroked her hair one last time before stepping back. "Good night, princess."

Settling onto the couch again a few moments later, he allowed his head to fall back against the cushions as he released a long, gusty breath. And then he straightened and reached for his notes again.

* * *

A week after she'd rushed out, Mia returned to Connor's house. She invited her brother to come in, but he declined, telling her he wanted to get back home before it got too late. They hugged tightly, silently celebrating, and then Paul drove away.

Carrying her bags, Mia let herself in the front door. She'd seen Connor's car in the carport beside her own, so she knew he was home. She'd called to tell him when she would arrive, so he wouldn't be surprised to see her.

The living room was empty when she walked in, but she heard sounds coming from the kitchen. Talking and laughter. Connor's and Alexis's voices. How she had missed them both, she thought with a clench in her throat.

She noted that the living room was very tidy. Maybe there was a little dust on the tables, but everything was in its place. Anxious to see Connor and Alexis, she left her bags sitting in the living room when she went in search of them.

She stopped in the kitchen doorway and felt her heart trip at the sight of them. Alexis wore one of Mia's aprons and was stirring something in a big bowl. A tea towel tucked into the belt of his jeans, Connor stood at the stove, ladling something from a steaming pan into a serving dish. The oven timer dinged and he reached for a potholder.

Alexis noticed Mia first. Dropping her spoon onto the table with a clatter, she pelted forward. "Mia, Mia! We've missed you."

Catching the child in her arms, Mia hugged her tightly. "I've missed you, too, sweetie. So much."

Connor set a pan of cornbread on a trivet before coming forward to greet her. His eyes searched her face, and she knew she looked tired and a little pale after her stressful week, but he said merely, "We're glad you're home. How's your dad?"

"He was doing well when I left. Glad to be home, of course, and already getting impatient to get back to his old routines. Mom's going to have her hands full making him follow all the doctor's orders, but I have no doubt she'll win the arguments. Carla's staying with them tonight, even though both Mom and Dad told her there was no need for her to do so."

"I'm glad to hear he's making such good progress."

"So am I," she said with a heartfelt nod. "He scared us all, but the doctors said if he takes care of himself and abides by their instructions, he should be almost fully recovered in a matter of weeks."

He looked at her mouth. She wondered if he was considering kissing her hello. She swallowed her disappointment when Alexis tugged at her shirt to reclaim her attention. "Mia, we made dinner for you. Daddy made chili and cornbread and he let me stir the dressing into a package of cold slaw."

"Coleslaw," Mia corrected automatically. "It all sounds delicious. I've had your daddy's chili before and he makes some of the best I've ever had."

Connor grinned and motioned toward the table. "Have a seat. I'll serve. I hope you're hungry."

"I'm starving."

It felt so good to be at the table with them again. Mia took a bite of thick, mildly spiced chili as she tried to listen to Alexis breathlessly reciting everything she had done in the week Mia had been away. Schoolwork, play dates with McKenzie, dance classes, a toy store and ice-cream outing with her daddy that morning.

"It sounds like you've had a busy week."

Alexis nodded, her mouth smeared with chili as she took a big bite of cornbread. Mia assumed Connor had made his signature dish much less spicy than usual for Alexis's sake. Normally Mia's mouth would be burning—in a good way—by now.

Taking advantage of his daughter having her mouth full to get in a few words of his own, Connor asked, "How's your mom, Mia?"

"She's fine, now that she knows Dad's going to be okay. I

told her I'd drive down next weekend to check on them again, but I think they'll be okay in the meantime. Carla and Paul will make sure of that."

"I got a new doll this morning, Mia," Alexis said after swallowing hastily. "Daddy bought her for me. Her name's Penny and she's going to be my new student."

Dragging her gaze from Connor's, Mia gave Alexis her full attention. "That sounds like fun. You'll have to show her to me after dinner."

Alexis claimed Mia's full attention for the remainder of the meal and the two hours after that. Connor remained quietly in the background, letting Mia and Alexis catch up. He opened his books to study while they admired the new doll and Mia saw all of Alexis's school papers from that week.

Bedtime came and Alexis gave Connor a big kiss before heading off to her room. "Mia will tuck me in tonight," she said.

He wasn't at all surprised. "Okay. Good night, princess. Sleep well."

"I will."

Turning, she tucked her hand into Mia's and skipped off.

He stood to pour himself a cup of coffee. He told himself he could relax now that Mia was back to take care of Alexis. The past week had been a challenge, but he had survived it. Now things could get back to the way they had been before.

Even as that thought crossed his mind, he knew it was bull. Go back to when? Before he and Mia had shared the first real kiss? Before they'd made love on that one perfect evening? Before he'd fallen in love with her? He'd have to go way back in time for that one, he thought glumly. He suspected that he'd been in love with Mia for a long time, although he'd been too stubborn and too deliberately distracted by other things to admit it.

Nothing could ever be the same. He only hoped that

whatever changes lay ahead for them, he wouldn't get his heart kicked around again. Brandy had bruised it, Gretchen had dented it, but only Mia had the power to shatter it.

"That smells good," she said from the doorway.

He glanced around. "You want a cup? It's not decaf, I'm afraid."

She hesitated, then shrugged. "Why not. Tomorrow's Sunday. I can relax then."

He poured a second cup for her. As he handed it to her, he thought back to the ice storm when a splashed cup of coffee had led to steaming kisses in the dark. He swallowed hard and turned half away. "We can take these into the living room."

She seemed to be having a little trouble meeting his eyes, too. "Fine."

He waited until she was seated on the couch, and then he settled beside her, placing his coffee cup on a coaster.

"How are you, really?" he asked, turning to face her. Studying the faint purple circles beneath her eyes, he wondered just how much rest she'd managed during the past week.

"I'm fine. A little tired, but just so glad Dad's going to be okay. He's only sixty-four. My family wasn't prepared to lose him yet."

"You're never ready," he murmured, thinking of his mother.

Shaking off the somber mood, she turned to look at him. "I felt terrible leaving you to deal with everything here on your own. I know you kept telling me everything was okay, but how did you manage?"

He smiled a little. "I'm not saying it was easy, but we got through it fine. Connie Porterfield was a great help. She took Alexis to dance classes and brought her home afterward. My study group met here several nights, so I didn't fall behind. We ate a lot of takeout, I'm afraid, but I tried to make healthy choices. I had a little trouble learning to tie a bow in Alexis's hair, but I'm getting pretty good at it, I think."

Her eyebrows rose. "It sounds like you managed quite well without me."

He gave a little shrug. "We got by."

She started to say something, but stopped with a frown, turning her head toward the doorway. "Did I hear Alexis?"

"Yeah, maybe—"

She moved to rise. "I'll go see what she—"

"Daddy!" The call came again, more clearly this time.

"Oh." Mia sank back into the cushions. "She wants you."

"I'll be right back."

He hurried toward Alexis's room, wondering what the problem could be. She hadn't been asleep long enough to have another nightmare, had she?

"What's up, princess?" he asked, opening her door and crossing the room.

Although she sounded a little drowsy, she wasn't asleep, and he didn't think she had been as yet. "Would you check under my bed?"

Tilting his head, he planted his fists on his hips. "You aren't afraid of anything under your bed," he accused her. He might not have been a father long, but he knew a con when he heard one.

"There could be something under there," she insisted, innocently batting her eyes.

"But there isn't and you know it." He reached down to tuck her covers more snugly beneath her chin, settling Pete and Bob beside her. "Go to sleep, princess. I'll be close by if you really need anything."

Maybe she had just wanted to hear that reassurance. Nestling into the pillow, she murmured, "Okay. 'Night, Daddy."

With a bemused shake of his head, he left the room to return to Mia.

Because Connor was smiling when he returned, Mia allowed herself to relax. "It wasn't a bad dream?"

He shook his head and sat beside her again. "Not this time.

She was just stalling. A variation on the old can-I-have-a-drink-of-water routine."

"Oh." She thought about that a moment. "She's never done that before."

"No. I used to try every excuse in the book to keep my parents coming into my room at night."

"Mia!"

Connor placed a hand on Mia's shoulder when she started to get up in response to the call. "Go to sleep, Alexis," he called out.

They could just hear the muttered response. "Okay."

They waited a moment, but when no further sound came from the direction of her room, Connor smiled. "See?"

Aware that his hand was still on her shoulder, she eyed his rather smug expression. "You're right. You are getting pretty good at this."

"Thanks."

Oddly enough, his increasing confidence gave her a funny little pang deep inside. Wasn't this what she'd wanted? For Connor to start taking more responsibility, gradually replacing her as Alexis's primary caretaker? So why was she suddenly feeling a little excluded?

"I think I've figured out what was causing the nightmares." Connor glanced toward the doorway and then back at Mia with a somber expression. "So many people have left her. She just needs occasional reassurance that someone's still here for her. That she can count on someone being there when she cries out. Someone to check under the bed for monsters," he added with a slight smile.

That was pretty much what she had surmised as well. "I always knew you could do this. Take care of Alexis and finish school, I mean. You see—you can handle much more than you thought you could."

He looked down at his hand on her shoulder and moved his thumb in a lazy circle that made a shiver run down her back. "I guess you were right," he murmured.

"I guess I was."

His eyes met hers again. "I missed you, Mia. Sure, I got by, but it wasn't the same without you here."

Her breath caught. "I know it's easier for you when I'm here to help."

"Easier?" He gave what might have been a short, skeptical laugh. "I'm not sure I would say that."

That made her frown. "I meant that I help you with Alexis. Help around the house."

"You do all those things and it's great. Gives me more time to focus on my studies. But as for easier—" He shook his head. "When you're here, it's all I can do to think about anything but you. The way I feel about you. The things I want to say to you."

She felt her breath catch.

He started to drop his hand. "I'm sorry. It's a bad time for me to—"

"No." She grabbed his hand, gripped it in hers as she stared fiercely into his eyes. "What is it you want to say?"

"You're tired. We can do this later."

She shook her head. "The one thing I've learned during the last week is that you never know if there will even be a later. We've been tiptoeing around each other for months and it's making us both miserable. We've always been honest with each other. The best of friends. I want that back."

His eyes darkened. She could almost feel him draw away from her, emotionally if not physically. "You want to just be friends. I'm not sure that's possible now, but we can try. I'll try to—"

"That isn't what I said," she interrupted impatiently. "We've always been more than 'just' friends. You are my *best* friend. The person who means more to me than anyone else in the world."

His head lifted, his eyes narrowing on her face. "What are you telling me, Mia?"

She drew a deep breath for courage, then spoke in a rush. "I've always been a giver. I enjoy taking care of my family and friends, doing everything I can to make sure they're happy. It gives me joy to see people I care about get what they want, achieve their goals and dreams. Sometimes I get so caught up in making other people happy that I forget to take care of my own needs. And there have been a few who have taken advantage of my generosity. Who have used me."

"Dale," he muttered with a scowl, referring to her brief relationship with a man Connor had disliked at first sight.

She kept her gaze steady on his. "Among others."

His hand jerked in hers. "Surely you aren't accusing me of being one of them."

Keeping her fingers tightly around his, she didn't look away. "No. You aren't anything like Dale. His only concern was what I had to offer him. He never really cared what I wanted or needed in return."

"I care," Connor said, his voice rough. "But you have to tell me what you need from me. I can't read your mind."

Her eyes burning, she nodded. "I realize that now. It's occurred to me that I didn't know whether you could give me what I wanted because I never told you what that was."

"Name it," he said huskily.

"I know you need me. I think you even love me," she murmured.

He reached out to lay his free hand over both of hers. "You should never doubt that."

"I need to know that you trust me."

He frowned, looking startled by her whisper. "What are you talking about? Of course I trust you."

"You trust me as a friend. You trust me with your daughter. Both very important. But do you trust me with your heart?"

"I don't know what—" He stopped, and she saw awareness come into his eyes.

Still gazing into his eyes, she said quietly, "Alexis isn't the only one who needs reassurance that someone will always be there. I think you've been struggling with the same fears."

She leaned closer to him, enunciating very clearly. "I'm not Brandy. And I'm not Gretchen. I love you. If you ask me to stay with you, I won't walk away from you when things get difficult or when I need to find myself."

His throat worked with a hard swallow. "I know you have plans…"

"Yes, I have plans. I'd like to start working toward a doctorate in American literature within the next year or two. Maybe I'd like to try teaching on a college level eventually. It's not a burning desire or I'd have started already. I enjoy teaching high school students and I haven't been in a big hurry to stop. But it's still my ultimate goal and I have every intention of pursuing it, whether I'm with you or on my own."

He sighed. "I'm going to be swamped with classes and schoolwork next year, preparing for the Step One exams. For two years after that, I'll be doing rotations, working and studying long hours. For the next three years after that, I'll be a medical resident. Long hours, relatively low pay. So for the next six foreseeable years, I don't know how much I can do to help you with your studies."

"Can you listen when I vent? Can you encourage me when I doubt myself? Can you celebrate with me when I do well, sympathize when things go wrong?"

"Of course I can do all that, but—"

"That's all I need from you," she said steadily. "We'll have to deal with the logistics of hectic schedules and child care and finances and all the other day-to-day details a busy family encounters. We'll have conflicts and challenges and victories and disappointments. And through all of that, Connor, I won't walk away. And I won't let *you* walk away either. Not if you tell me right now that you love me and you trust me."

His hands tightened around hers. "I love you."

"And—?"

"And I—I trust you."

"Enough to ask me to stay with you for always?"

"I don't want you to feel tied down—"

She sighed and asked again, "Do you trust me enough to ask me to stay?"

There was a long pause during which she found it difficult to breathe. Had he been hurt too badly to ever take another risk on love? Was he so focused on his own plans that he just didn't think he had enough of himself left to give? Could he…?

"Stay, Mia."

Her heart tripped. "Say that again."

His smile was so sweet, his eyes so tender that her own filled with tears. "I love you. Stay with me. Be a family with me and Alexis. I'll be your cheerleader. I'll be your shoulder to cry on. I'll be anything you need from me. Just promise you'll stay."

"And if I make that promise?" she whispered.

"Then I'll believe you," he replied steadily. Confidently. "Just as you can believe that I'm not going anywhere either. You're my best friend. You always will be."

With a happy sob, she went into his arms, fitting her smiling lips to his own.

Epilogue

The wedding took place on the first Saturday in June. Because both the bride and groom had very busy schedules, the ceremony was a simple one. It was held beside the lake at Mia's parents' vacation home on a warm, clear afternoon, attended by her family and closest friends, Connor's study group and a few old friends of his.

Mia wore her mother's fitted sheath wedding dress and carried a bouquet of red roses. Connor wore a dark suit. Natalie served as maid of honor, Duncan Hayes stood as his son's best man and Alexis was an adorable flower girl in a lace-trimmed white dress with a flowing red ribbon. Following the ceremony, the guests dined at tables set up on the lawn, serenaded by music from hidden outdoor speakers.

As far as Mia was concerned, it was the most beautiful wedding ever.

"You look so happy," her mother said with tears in her eyes after the vows were exchanged.

Mia laughed and looked at her husband, who was dancing across the grass with his laughing daughter held high in his arms. "Why wouldn't I be happy? I just married my best friend."

Gazing at her own best friend and husband of more than thirty years, who looked healthy and content as he chatted with their guests, her mother sighed contentedly. Following the direction of her mom's attention, Mia smiled, so grateful that her father had been there to walk with her to where Connor and the officiate had waited.

"Mia." Alexis looked her way, beckoning eagerly. "Come dance with us."

Connor looked her way, too, his smile loving, his handsome face more relaxed than she had seen him in a long time. "Yes, Mia. Come dance with us."

Laughing, Mia kissed her mom's soft cheek, then hurried happily across the lawn to join her husband and the little girl who had made their lives so complete.

* * * * *

RICK'S APPOINTMENT with his attorney early Wednesday morning went only moderately better than his meeting with social services the day before. The prognosis wasn't great—but at least his attorney was going to file a motion for DNA testing. Just so Rick could petition to see the child…his sister's baby. The sister he didn't know he had until it was too late.

The rest of what his attorney said had been downhill from there.

Cell phone in hand before he'd even reached his Nitro, Rick punched in the speed dial number he'd programmed the day before.

Maybe foster parent Sue Bookman hadn't received his message. Or had lost his number. Maybe she didn't want to talk to him. At this point he didn't much care what she wanted.

"Hello?" She answered before the first ring was complete. And sounded breathless.

Young and breathless.

"Ms. Bookman?"

"Yes. This is Rick Kraynick, right?"

"Yes, ma'am."

"I recognized your number on caller ID," she said, her voice uneven, as though she was still engaged in whatever physical activity had her so breathless to begin with. "I'm sorry I didn't get back to you. I've been a little…distracted."

The words came in more disjointed spurts. Was she jogging?

"No problem," he said, when, in fact, he'd spent the better part of the night before watching his phone. And fretting. "Did I get you at a bad time?"

"No worse than usual," she said, adding, "Better than some. So, how can I help?"

God, if only this could be so easy. He'd ask. She'd help. And life could go well. At least for one little person in his family.

It would be a first.

"Mr. Kraynick?"

"Yes. Sorry. I was… Are you sure there isn't a better time to call?"

"I'm bouncing a baby, Mr. Kraynick. It's what I do."

"Is it Carrie?" he asked quickly, his pulse racing.

"How do you know Carrie?" She sounded defensive, which wouldn't do him any good.

"I'm her uncle," he explained, "her mother's—Christy's— older brother, and I know you have her."

"I can neither confirm nor deny your allegations, Mr. Kraynick. Please call social services." She rattled off the number.

"Wait!" he said, unable to hide his urgency. "Please," he said more calmly. "Just hear me out."

"How did you find me?"

"A friend of Christy's."

"I'm sorry I can't help you, Mr. Kraynick," she said softly. "This conversation is over."

"I grew up in foster care," he said, as though that gave him some special privilege. Some insider's edge.

"Then you know you shouldn't be calling me at all."

"Yes… But Carrie is my niece," he said. "I need to see her. To know that she's okay."

"You'll have to go through social services to arrange that."

"I'm sure you know it's not as easy as it sounds. I'm a single man with no real ties and I've no intention of petitioning for custody. They aren't real eager to give me the time of day. I never even knew Carrie's mother. For all intents and purposes, our mother didn't raise either one of us. All I have going for me is half a set of genes. My lawyer's on it, but it could be weeks—months—before this is sorted out. Carrie could be adopted by then. Which would be fine, great for her, but then I'd have lost my chance. I don't want to take her. I won't hurt her. I just have to see her."

"I'm sorry, Mr. Kraynick, but…"

* * * * *

Find out if Rick Kraynick will ever have
a chance to meet his niece.
Look for A DAUGHTER'S TRUST by Tara Taylor Quinn,
available in September 2009.

We'll be spotlighting a different series every month throughout 2009 to celebrate our 60th anniversary.

Look for Harlequin® Superromance® in September!

Celebrate with The Diamond Legacy miniseries!

Follow the stories of four cousins as they come to terms with the complications of love and what it means to be a family. Discover with them the sixty-year-old secret that rocks not one but two families.

A DAUGHTER'S TRUST by *Tara Taylor Quinn*
September

FOR THE LOVE OF FAMILY by *Kathleen O'Brien*
October

LIKE FATHER, LIKE SON by *Karina Bliss*
November

A MOTHER'S SECRET by *Janice Kay Johnson*
December

Available wherever books are sold.

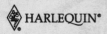

You're invited to join our Tell Harlequin Reader Panel!

By joining our new reader panel you will:

- Receive Harlequin® books—they are FREE and yours to keep with no obligation to purchase anything!
- Participate in fun online surveys
- Exchange opinions and ideas with women just like you
- Have a say in our new book ideas and help us publish the best in women's fiction

In addition, you will have a chance to win great prizes and receive special gifts!
See Web site for details. Some conditions apply.
Space is limited.

To join, visit us at
www.TellHarlequin.com.

REQUEST YOUR FREE BOOKS!

2 FREE NOVELS PLUS 2 FREE GIFTS!

SPECIAL EDITION®

Life, Love and Family!

Stay up-to-date on all your romance reading news!

The Harlequin
Inside Romance
newsletter is a **FREE**
quarterly newsletter
highlighting
our upcoming
series releases
and promotions!

Go to
eHarlequin.com/InsideRomance
or e-mail us at
InsideRomance@Harlequin.com
to sign up to receive
your **FREE** newsletter today!

You can also subscribe by writing to us at: HARLEQUIN BOOKS
Attention: Customer Service Department
P.O. Box 9057, Buffalo, NY 14269-9057

Please allow 4-6 weeks for delivery of the first issue by mail.

IRNBPAQ209

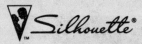
Silhouette®

COMING NEXT MONTH
Available August 25, 2009

#1993 TEXAS CINDERELLA—Victoria Pade
The Foleys and the McCords
When Tate McCord caught reporter Tanya Kimbrough snooping around the McCord mansion for business secrets, he had to admit—the housekeeper's daughter had become a knockout! The real scoop—this Texas Cinderella was about to steal the surgeon's heart.

#1994 A MARRIAGE-MINDED MAN—Karen Templeton
Wed in the West
Lasting relationships had never been in the cards for single mom Tess Montaya. But when her teenage sweetheart, Eli Garrett, reentered her life, it looked as if this time they were playing for keeps. Could the carpenter and the Realtor build a home…together?

#1995 THE PREGNANT BRIDE WORE WHITE—
Susan Crosby
The McCoys of Chance City
When Keri Overton came to Chance City to tell Jake McCoy he was going to be a daddy, he wasn't there. But the town gave her such a warm welcome, she stayed…until Jake returned, in time for nine-months-pregnant Keri to make an honest man of him.

#1996 A COLD CREEK HOMECOMING—RaeAnne Thayne
The Cowboys of Cold Creek
Home visiting his ailing mother, CEO Quinn Sutherland was shocked to find snooty ol' Tess Clayborne caring for her. In high school, Quinn had thought the homecoming queen was stuck up—but now he found the softer, gentler woman irresistible….

#1997 BABY BY SURPRISE—Karen Rose Smith
The Baby Experts
As a neonatologist, Francesca Talbot knew a thing or two about babies—until it came to her own difficult pregnancy. That's when she turned to the child's father, rancher Grady Fitzgerald, to provide shelter in the storm…and a love to last a lifetime.

#1998 THE HUSBAND SHE COULDN'T FORGET—
Carmen Green
Abandoned by her husband, Melanie Bishop took a job as a therapist…and immediately fell for her amnesiac patient Rolland Jones, whom a car accident had transformed inside and out. What was it about Rolland that reminded her so of the husband she'd loved?

SSECNMBPA0809